Books by George Ovitt

Poetry
Splitting the Difference
What Happens Next
*

Short Stories
The Snowman
*

Novels
Stillpoint
Tribunal
*

History
The Restoration of Perfection

Tribunal
A Novel

George Ovitt

Fomite
Burlington, VT

ISBN-13: 978-1-944388-85-0
Library of Congress Control Number: 2019940228
Fomite
58 Peru Street
Burlington, VT 05401

In memory of
David F. Noble

"When we roll out clichés like 'time will tell' and 'the judg-ment of history,' we are of course playing with language. Time does not speak, nor does history judge."
—John W. Dower, *Cultures of War*

"We are never capable of interpreting for ourselves."
—Imre Kertész, *Fiasco*

"In the first days of March, 1970, a rumor circulated around Phnom Penh that a white crocodile had been sighted near the capital. The story spread quickly…His appearances above ground only occur when the Cambodian people are at a crossroads."

—Elizabeth Becker, *When the War Was Over:*
Cambodia and the Khmer Rouge Revolution

Prologue

February 3, 2012

They often have an alias. A *nom de guerre*. This is a part of the romance; not hiding, but boasting: *you see, I am a new person, a better human being, born again.* And they look like us—nondescript. Yet, with what we know, the faces of these three are grotesque—masks of evil. The monsters of Cambodia's immolation insist upon their normality. In photographs taken in the twentieth century, at the moment when they were murdering three million of their countrymen, the leaders of the Khmer Rouge—Ta Mok and Pol Pot and Khieu Samphan—look like happy peasants. Pleased at the thought of the bodies of their enemies, enamored of their ideas, sure of themselves.

Pol Pot always smiled for the camera. The three look disarmingly average. Not banal. That was a poor choice of words. Evil can never be banal, though evildoers may appear so.

It's Friday, February 3, 2012. It's cold in this city, bitter cold, but clear. There was a full moon last night. Extraordinary as it rose over the mountains. My thoughts are as vivid as this clear sky—a blue turquoise emptiness the color of Navaho jewelry, my mind transformed into transparency, my thoughts oxygenated, my dreams hallucinatory.

It is evening, though the days have lengthened perceptibly. I walked home from work—three miles, difficult at my age, but I no longer drive. Each day I listen to the radio, to a station that broadcasts a news program hosted by a woman who appears to tell the truth. She spoke today about the trials of those accused in Cambodia of 'crimes against humanity,' a term I dislike for its neutrality, but it is the term *en vogue*. As I walked I was startled to hear names I haven't heard for over thirty years. The names of the rulers of Cambodia in the 1970s. A part of my life came back the moment I heard *Tuol Sleng*. And 'Duch'.

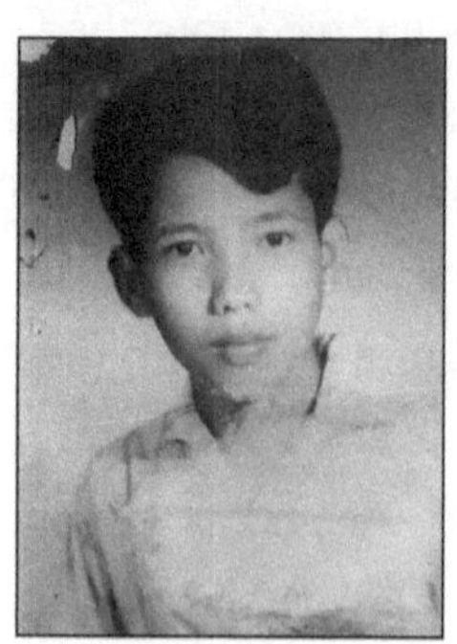

Like Kang Kek Leu, I am a teacher. I talk to young people about history, a hopeless task, as the past no longer exists. As truth no longer exists. We live in a perpetual present, like the Buddhists of No-Mind, and the images of Kang Kek Leu, alias Duch, alias Hang Pin or "ghost" in Khmer, the master of the torture center known as S-21, a former French lycée, can only be collected from most obscure corners of the Internet. But there he was—on my portable radio. The *Times* will mention that the verdict reached in Duch's case—life in prison—was handed down today. In Albuquerque knowledge of this fact will be esoteric, like knowledge of the Names of God or the order of Chinese dynasties. No one I encounter during my day—no one I meet in my life—will care about the verdict. It is, in the language of the moment, a "data point." The anti-climax is palpable, but everything has faded to anti-climax. I am absolutely certain that if a bomb were to be detonated on the endless empty plains south of the city no one would take notice—we consume amnesia with the thin air and arsenic-tainted water.

In his first sermon—*Dhammacakkappavattana-sutta*, or "setting into motion the wheel of Dharma,"—the Buddha advised his followers to renounce the thirst for life, to renounce the thirst for death, to renounce the thirst for pleasure and pain. To renounce all things. Reading this sermon for the first time, many years ago, I laughed out loud, finding such nihilism absurd and responding in a facile way to what was beyond my imagining. Now I understand what the Buddha meant, though I am not yet prepared to act upon this knowledge. My thirst is still too deep, and rather than renunciation, the radio report awakens in me a host of emotions—grief to be sure, but anger, curiosity, and the desire to remember.

I live in a plain, affordable apartment. I have two bedrooms, a small kitchen, and a living room. The complex is called "Vista del Arroyo." An *arroyo* is a ditch that sluices rainwater from the monsoons of summer westward, down the foothills and into the valley that ends in the Rio Grande, a muddy slip of water that reminds me of the Mekong. I always arrive home shortly after 6 p.m. On weekends, apart from long walks, I remain at home. When I arrive at my apartment after work I feel the emptiness of the rooms. No visitor has set foot in my apartment for twelve years. And yet my situation is in most respects highly advantageous. My health is good, my finances are tolerable, and I have mostly settled my accounts with the past. When I left the East for Albuquerque I did so to start over, just as so many millions of us have crossed the Mississippi to begin anew. Two centuries ago, Meriwether Lewis wrote from Camp DuBois in the Illinois Territory that the continent "stretched out like a great dream of what a man could be," and I felt something like that promise when I drove for first time across the bridge connecting East and West St. Louis—dire poverty on the east side of the river, and, above the glistening brown water, the shadow of the arch, pulling me to the West where, like Lewis, I would one day dream of what I could be.

I put a record of Frank Morgan's on the stereo. He performed here in Albuquerque in the autumn, with

George Cables and a drummer who was very good. I bought a front row ticket and was transfixed as Morgan played the standards. Frank played sitting down, and, though the night was cool and room airy, he perspired through his white dashiki.

Few things in life are as gratifying as witnessing someone do something well. This is true in any field of human endeavor; perhaps this is what Aristotle meant by achieving the 'good,' not just doing something well, but transcending the thing itself, so that playing jazz or hitting a fastball or writing poetry becomes a manifestation of the Good itself, a higher state of being than any enjoyed in ordinary life. On the stereo Morgan is playing "You Must Believe in Spring."

Throughout his trial, Duch insisted on his innocence. His defense was focused on the claim that he was not a key operative in the Khmer Rouge, merely a lackey of Pol Pot. This is a lie, but it is the preferred lie of all mass murderers and their accomplices. Duch was among the founding fathers of the movement to end Cambodia's bourgeois history. The historical record suggests that Duch relished his job, that he exerted himself to eliminate the enemies of the new Khmer Republic. Tens of thousands of Cambodians—men, women, and children—were incarcerated, interrogated, tortured, and murdered in S-21.

I wonder at the utilitarian name. Why not S-23?

I have thought about S-21 now and then ever since I first heard about it, thirty years ago. That seems like a long time to think about something so mundane, and of course I have thought about lots of other things as well. Mostly, when people say that they have *given something some thought,* they usually mean it has *crossed their mind.* S-21, and Duch, and the Khmer Rouge have done much more than *cross my mind.* These words, their meanings, the images evoked by them have driven fissures as deep as these *arroyos* into my brain, roadways of association that carry a weight of feeling that I struggle with, mostly without success. Part of what has drawn me back to S-21 is my need to re-live events of which I was a part. I was in Cambodia during the last years of its existence. You could say I was a guilty bystander, perhaps even a participant, in the destruction of that country. I have an explanation of these events, but this explanation adds up to zero.

When I walk home, I watch the changing light on the west-facing slope of the mountains. Granite and basalt glows orange in the winter evenings, and I enjoy the play of light on the rock, the complexity of the refraction that bends into indigo and violet. The flat plane of the northernmost peak reminds me of Monet's vision of Rouen Cathedral, the great tower, dabs of mauve pigment blending into the receding sky.

This is a large city, but in winter I feel like the only man alive, as if everyone has disappeared into one of the alien spacecraft said to hover above the desert. The first time I saw this city was in the 1970s. At that time it was a small town of 40,000. Many areas of the city, especially nearer the mountains, had only dirt roads, and when I visited, in the middle of the summer, a shroud of dust obscured the meager skyline. I had driven south from my home in Philadelphia, through western Georgia and across the northern hills of Alabama and Mississippi. Camping outside of Oxford, Mississippi, I sat in my tent, fending off mosquitos, reading a biography of Huey Long and sipping ice tea. On a day-long tour of Rowen Oak, Faulkner's melancholy home, a white ramshackle house shrouded by magnolia and tupelo, I paced across the disheveled grounds, looking for some physical sign of the great writer and thinking about what he saw as he made the rounds himself. In his honor, I sat on a log in view of the back porch, drank a half-pint of Jim Beam, and read the last few pages of *Absalom, Absalom* aloud in the humid air. I then drove into the Ozark Mountains and hiked along hilly trails that overlooked unbroken forest. The South was a foreign country, a place I couldn't imagine even when I was there. The air smelled of sulfur. Everywhere there were hand-lettered signs advertising pecans, watermelon, and revival meetings. The towns, bustling in the early morning, were deserted by mid-day as the asphalt fried in the heat. Black people lived in shacks along narrow tar roads that led from one hamlet to another. It rained every afternoon, and by the time I crossed the border into Oklahoma my clothes and sleeping bag were mildewed and my guts were churning from weak coffee and fried food. I drove all night until I came to Raton, high above the grassy plain that sweeps down from the front-range of the Rockies into eastern New Mexico. The air was crisp and dry, the towns spread across miles of busy highways that rumbled day and night under the weight of immense trucks pulling horse trailers, cattle, and bales of alfalfa. I felt right at home. It was the emptiness that drew me in, that propelled me further south, down the flatlands into Santa Rosa, and then across the enormous midsection of the desert to Albuquerque. I stayed a week, switching from one quaint Route 66 motel to another, settling finally into La Vada, a ten unit, 40s motor-court that reminded me of family trips along Route 301 from New York to Florida. The back units were reserved for hookers, and the manager told me that if I didn't mind the regular trade I could take the next-to-last room for a discount. They built solid walls in the years after the war, cinder block and stucco rather than plaster. I slept like a baby as the johns came and went. In the morning, late, a couple of bedraggled blondes sat in Adirondack chairs in front of their room smoking and nipping at a bottle of vodka. I introduced myself and asked if I could buy them a doughnut from Don's Donut Bar. They said they didn't eat in the morning, but we got to talking, and I learned about the life they lived on the east end of Central Avenue. The older of the two was named Barbara—she told me she was twenty-six but Connie, her friend, rolled her eyes at this lie. They warned me not to go further than Washington Street if I took a walk.

I stayed at the La Vada for a week, smoking and gossiping with the women in the mornings, driving around the city, walking the mountain trails, eating cheap food at cafés by the University. It was a good week for me. I felt right at home under the blue sky, with the vast empty plains beckoning me to get in my truck and drive to the West coast, to gaze on the Pacific Ocean and to imagine myself crossing it again, on my way to Cam Ranh Bay.

The point is that you remember times like these later on in life; ordinary days when you don't do anything but live.

On the radio, there was talk by Duch's lawyers of the "violations of his rights." One lawyer questioned the notion of a "crime against humanity," making a Scholastic-sounding argument about the difficulty of defining "humanity." I was perplexed as I listened. The law can be infuriating in its even-handed disregard of simple moral truths. It wasn't humanity that was tortured, but human beings. I thought for the ten thousandth time of the vast difference between the general and the particular, the pointlessness of abstractions. I went on my computer to look at his face. He was still smiling. Why wasn't he ashamed? Under the circumstances one would expect modesty, or a serious demeanor. No. Duch grins at the camera, a broad-faced man with graying hair and bad teeth.

My neighbors are mostly unmarried women with small children. Mrs. Menendez next door has two daughters, aged nine and six, and once every few weeks she will ask me to watch them while she goes to Walmart. Mrs. Menendez speaks only Spanish, but her girls are bilingual. The three of us sit on the couch in their crowded apartment and read books that I borrow from my school's well-stocked library. I have been reading L.M. Montgomery's novel *Anne of Green Gables* to Rita and Esmeralda for the past two months.

Nothing could be further from the experience of these two children than the life of Prince Edward Island at the turn of the twentieth century. On the other hand, Anne was an orphan, and Rita and Esmeralda—and Mrs. Menendez herself—are orphans in our strange, unforgiving country. Mrs. Menendez is a secretary at the local public school. The father of her children is in prison in Los Lunas for possession of methamphetamines. Mrs. Menendez is a Catholic and doesn't believe in divorce. Her husband will be free in eight more years, with time off for good behavior, whatever that means. So the children will grow up without a father. When we sit together on Mrs. Menendez's couch, they lean against me to look at the book, though there are no pictures. They are smaller than most children their age. Mrs. Menendez lacks the resources, or perhaps the knowledge of nutrition, that wealthier parents appear to possess, almost as a birthright. I have noticed many pizza boxes in their trash. Rita, the eldest, asked me if I could take her and Esmeralda ice-skating at the Outpost. I asked Mrs. Menendez if I might, but she told me that it wouldn't be a good idea.

Duch stood, I understand from the broadcast, "impassively, without emotion" as his sentence was read by the judge. He can appeal in seven years, but otherwise the judgment rendered today is final. Initially Duch had been sentenced to thirty-five years, with sixteen years subtracted from his sentence for time served. The prosecutors appealed what they considered a too lenient sentence for the murder of 16,000 people. On the radio, a commentator tells the host "justice has been served." I was crossing Academy

Boulevard when I heard this phrase and I stopped, right in the middle of the street. What do these words mean? Are we Platonists, worrying about the service of Justice? Then, as I reached the meridian, safe for a moment from the race of traffic, I thought—what should the punishment be for the murder of 16,000 people? Perhaps the thing to do would be to let Duch go, or to let him live in a villa, with servants—why not? Irony might be best in this case. Imagine the judge saying, "Mr. Duch, let's not worry about it. It's water under the bridge." There must be a Khmer equivalent of this liberal sentiment. "Mistakes were made. No one blames you. Let bygones be bygones. You break a few eggs…" Maybe not that one. But the idea is refreshing, American. There's no reason to feel too bad about such things. Time marches on. And, really, who cares?

Mrs. Menendez changed her mind. Or perhaps Rita wore her down. Two Saturdays ago the four of us boarded the L Route bus and rode up Montgomery to Tramway where we changed to the R. After a long, silent ride—the girls sat with me, leaving Mrs. Menendez alone in front of us—we reached the Outpost. I paid the admission fee and the skate rental—nearly fifty dollars—and walked out onto the ice with Rita and Esmeralda. I was a skillful skater as a boy, but now even walking around the rink is diffi-cult. I slid around on my skates as the girls wobbled and giggled their way through the crowd. Esmeralda called me "*El Pulgarcito*" as I shuffled across the slushy ice. It hadn't occurred to me that I would be so beloved by these children—"little thumb," a term of endearment, or so it seemed to me. Mrs. Menendez, not athletic herself, sat staring at the numbing whirl of skaters, probably wishing she could smoke. I waved to her as we turned the corner, but she ignored me, thinking perhaps of her incarcerated husband. On the bus ride home, Esmeralda fell asleep on my arm. When we arrived at Vista del Arroyo, Mrs. Menendez picked up her little girl, smiled half-heartedly at me, and strode up the stairs to her apartment. As usual, the human heart mystified me. Yet I have known enough of living to understand that no one is able to express what she truly feels. As she went inside her apartment, Rita turned and waved.

In a file cabinet in my apartment, and on the walls full of books, I keep my notebooks, cheap, marble-covered, college ruled, two-hundred page repositories of my past, blank pages on which, for years, I scribbled notes on my reading, on the events of my life, on my muddled thoughts. There are hundreds of them, identical, an army of memory. The earliest ones go back to 1968; they continue right up to the present. The first sentence in the first book reads as follows: "I do not intend to allow my life to go unrecorded." When I wrote that sentence I was staying at the YMCA on Wabash Street in Chicago. I had just quit college and taken a train to a city where I knew no one, but which attracted me for its perch on Lake Michigan and for the blues clubs on Wells Street. I bought the notebook in Klein's Stationary Store on Cicero. Thanks to the note I made on that day forty-three years ago I can recollect the worn plank floor of Klein's, the rows of notebooks and pens, boxes of envelopes stacked on a black wire racks around the wall, mucilage—a word I love—in tiny brown bottles. And in the front of the store, a man, the eponymous Mr. Klein I supposed, a dapper old guy wearing a bow tie and vest, his thin graying hair parted in just the way my grandfather parted his hair, high up on the scalp, giving the appearance of jauntiness, an effect my grandfather cultivated but which seemed misplaced on Mr. Klein. The counter was rubbed smooth by ten thousand transactions, the cash register a monster of filigreed iron, with little off-white panels carrying the numbers, ones and tens separated by a decimal dot, the mechanical whirring of gears as prices were punched onto the keys, and a gratifying *kerchanging* as the numbers rose behind the dirty glass. I still have the receipt, hand-written by Mr. Klein, long dead I fear, his store now a thrift shop or worse. One notebook, one Parker refillable ballpoint, a box of Eagle pencils and a Snickers bar. Three dollars and sixty-five cents, with tax. A gratifying commercial transaction, as I recall it now. I had a need, not pressing, but worthy enough to be fulfilled, and Mr. Klein had the things I needed. All of this is written in my miniscule handwriting on the first two pages of the notebook numbered with the Roman numeral 'I,' a system I kept up until I arrived at my fortieth book, when I switched to Arabic—or is it Indian?—numerals, having forgotten how to proceed after XXXIX; and now these pages are brown and crumbly like oak leaves pressed in glass. There is something lovely in such a memory, as rich in its way as my first kiss, which, because it came before I began my obsessive writing, I have forgotten.

A year later, almost to the day, I was in Vietnam.

The woman on the radio, the one I listen to every afternoon, has a calm, sympathetic voice. I imagine her sitting in a studio in New York, surrounded by microphones and video screens and technical equipment, reading words that pass through the stratosphere, across the Great Plains and against the revolution of the earth—I imagine storms and banks of clouds, jets hurtling east and west toward cities I have never visited—her words coded into bits of electronic buzz, and then, after an infinitesimal moment, finding their way into my dollar-sized radio, vibrating the tympani of my ears, being turned into pulses of nerve—my inner network a duplicate of hers—and making their way to my auditory cortex—symbols, arbitrary sounds, stirring memories of being deployed along the Ho Chi Minh trail in eastern Cambodia in 1970, and also memories of a person I spent some hours with in Philadelphia thirty years ago. The radio woman's voice reminds me of my mother's voice when *she* was a young woman, or, rather, when I first knew her. But she *was* young. I was born when my mother was twenty-six. She was a lovely girl then, with long brown hair and laughing eyes. She had many boyfriends in high school, and even more, apparently, during the War, when she worked as a telephone switchboard operator at Ft. Monmouth in central New Jersey. I have a box of photos that she mailed me a few weeks before she died. Most of the pictures were ones I had never seen. In some she is obviously posing—several in swimsuits, the long loose kind, fashionable on the Jersey Shore in the early 40s. In others taken, I think, by a professional photographer, she is surrounded by three handsome young men in a soda fountain, drinking an ice cream soda, her favorite dessert even when I came at last to know her. One so seldom thinks of one's parents' lives before they had children. My mother and I walked hand in hand on Second Avenue to the boardwalk where I was allowed two rides—two rides for ten cents—and then we would stroll toward the Casino to Harold's for black and whites. This is a memory I have not needed to write down until now. The young men in the photograph are smiling. One is wearing a beanie and a high school letter sweater. He looks a little like my father looked back then, but it wasn't him. When my mother was dying she called to tell me that she was happy to go. "I'm happy to go," were her exact words, as if she were embarking on a trip to Paris, a city she had always wanted to visit. And I said, "Please don't go yet." I didn't want to cry. It is bad manners to weep among the dying; one must be cheerful. And she said nothing. In fact, she was silent for so long I thought she had hung up. I finally said, "Mom, are you there?" "Unfortunately."

Just after the report on Duch's sentencing, as I was making my way up through the park that borders Vista del Arroyo, the reporter I trust signed off in her usual breathless way, reading a list of credits that meant nothing but which indicated that her producers subscribe to a policy of diversity in hiring, when, before I could switch my radio off, the bland male voice of a financial reporter signed on with the stock quotes that have become the index of American well-being. The market, he says, was up, the news was good, or bad, depending on which set of partisan illusions you subscribe to—good if you vote for false hope, bad if you prefer imminent apocalypse. I switched my radio off and stood for a long time watching one of the local high school soccer teams run their drills. There were small orange cones laid out on the immense grassy slope of the park—a suburban insult to the surrounding desert. Young men and women pushed balls through the cones with gentle skill. When I let my eyes leave the weaving players, when I looked up into the cottonwoods, I could see the contrails of three jets miles above me as they flew in parallel toward the East. A bit of snow lingered on the crest of the mountains after the January thaw—more snow was forecast for the weekend. The coach was yelling at the players—"switch, switch"— with the urgency that attaches itself to the insignificant. I thought of the people in the planes and wondered, as I always do, what they could see of us if they were to look up from their magazines and mystery novels. It has been many years since I was on an airplane, but I can remember the vast brown-green grid of the country below me giving way after many hours to the empty blue-green of the sea, the illusion of clarity giving way to an emptiness as great as the mind can conceive. The earth rotating, and the aluminum cylinder, dusted by clouds and the roar of air—that great sea of gases shrouding the earth, holding it in place— propelling me across the Pacific to Vietnam.

At the trial in Phnom Penh, someone read these words: "Duch oversaw a *precise department of death*." The phrase stuck with me. And then: "His guards dutifully photographed the prisoners upon arrival and photographed them at or near death, whether their throats were slit, their bodies mutilated, or so thin from torture and near starvation that they were beyond recognition." I have wondered about the tendency of psychopaths—whether working alone or as part of a government effort—to record their crimes. After much thought, I concluded that record-keeping is a dimension of cruelty that has been underestimated by historians and novelists. Murderers are as prone to forgetfulness as the rest of us. Who better than a provincial schoolteacher to take care not to lose the historic moment? After all, the Khmer Rouge was creating a worldly paradise to replace the old, corrupt human world. Pol Pot spoke in just that way: *the Paradise to come.* It is best not to dwell on such things, but the soccer players' precision and concentration puts me in mind of the role that ritual and boundless, ill-founded hope plays in our lives. *"A precise department of death."*

When I moved to the high desert in 2000, I didn't have a job, but I did have my disability pension from the Army. It wasn't much, but I had been living on it for years. I needed a place that was warm and inexpensive. America has one exceptional quality—no one cares if you pack up and move on. In fact, that's really the whole point—we are a nation of vagabonds, malcontents, and desperate seekers. I looked at a map in my small Philadelphia apartment. Where to? Low humidity, empty spaces, sunshine, cheap housing. When I arrived in Albuquerque and rented my apartment I settled into a routine that was satisfactory in every respect. I took long walks as a way to keep my legs limber and my mind alive. The landscape was invigorating. I hadn't known many people in Philadelphia, so my isolation required no adjustments. Shortly after I arrived some medical complications led to a stay in the hospital—the VA covered most of my costs, but not all, and for the first time in my life I was in need of funds. Though I never finished college, I have had a lifelong interest in languages and speak a couple. Inquires at the University led to part-time tutoring jobs, and then, fortuitously, to a job at the high school where I now teach. It turns out that I have a gift for talking to young people, perhaps because I am honest, or because the passage of years has unclenched my heart.

Since the point of this narrative isn't Cambodia, or not only Cambodia, and is only marginally about me, I should come to the point.

It wasn't only Duch who crossed my mind today. I also thought of Alice Turley. Perhaps because of my lingering nostalgia for the East, I continue to scan the Philadelphia newspapers on my computer. This morning, just after 7 a.m., sitting in my office sipping coffee, I found, quite by chance, this obituary, dated February 1, 2012:

A woman, identified as Alice Nye Turley, was found dead in her home in Mullica yesterday.
Mrs. Turley apparently died of natural causes.
Although reclusive in her later years, Mrs. Turley was well

known as an advocate for the Vietnamese and Cambodian citizens of the Philadelphia-South Jersey region. Most notably, Mrs. Turley appeared as a prominent witness in a 'trial' of those accused of crimes against humanity in Cambodia during the period of the Vietnam War. The trial was conducted under the auspices of the 'American Committee in Solidarity with Cambodia' in Washington, D.C. in 1978, and became an international event when Mrs. Turley and other members of the Committee challenged the Carter administration to live up to its commitment to human rights by bringing to justice at the International Court of Human Rights those accused of the crime of genocide in Cambodia, including Pol Pot, the leader of the Khmer Rouge during the period in question.

Mrs. Turley was a prominent speaker and writer on the subject of human rights in Southeast Asia, and Cambodia in particular, and the author of a well-received book, Cambodia: The Death of a Nation, *published in 1989. She taught for a decade at Montclair State College and at Drexel University. In recent years Mrs. Turley had retired to her family home in southern New Jersey, outside Mullica, where she continued her advocacy for the people of Cambodia. Mrs. Turley undertook several fact-finding trips to Southeast Asia on behalf of the ACSC, but was never permitted to reenter Cambodia. She published a second book,* Testimonies from The 'Killing Fields', *in 1990. Ben Norton, writing in the* New York Times, *called the book, "An extraordinary homage to the lives of ordinary men and women who perished in the Cambodian genocide."*

Mrs. Turley was born in Mullica in 1948, attended local schools in Hammonton as well as Georgetown University. She worked for the State Department in Cambodia in the early 1970s, retiring from that agency after her evacuation from Cambodia in 1975.

She married Philip Turley, of Cambridge, Massachusetts, in 1969; they were divorced in 1976.

There are no surviving family members.

I met Alice Turley on January 20, 1981. We spoke for an hour in the stairwell of the second basement floor of the Van Pelt Library at the University of Pennsylvania. We took a walk and had a cup of tea and some food. We also spoke—with considerable animation on her part—during the walk. Later in the day we went back to her apartment, had dinner, talked until the middle of the night, and then went to sleep. In the morning we walked to the campus, and on the front steps of the Van Pelt Library, the place where I spent each of my days, we said goodbye. I've never seen her since that day, though I have thought of her many times since. We had a great deal in common: we were both survivors of the catastrophe in Southeast Asia, scarred by two wars, and, perhaps as a consequence, alone in the world. Our rapport wasn't immediate. I was quiet, and Alice was aloof, but when she learned a little about me, and understood that I was interested in her life, she opened up and told me a great deal about herself. 'Vulnerable' and 'obsessed' were the words that came to mind as we spoke, at least that is what I wrote in my notebook that day. I also wrote the following sentences, recovered from one of my memory books:

"What does it mean to 'give oneself over' to a cause, to so fully empathize with another as to blot out one's own being? There are

ghosts in the world, beings that are not living here and now, and not living for themselves. They are spirits—the ones who remind us of uncomfortable truths." This is cryptic, but I was writing about Alice, and she embodied to a remarkable extent the Buddha's idea of lovingkindness.

When I met her, Alice was about to leave graduate school, where she had been hiding. I was relieved to learn that she was leaving Philadelphia, afraid that if she were to stay I would have to "deal with her." I'm not sure what this phrase means, but even now, I remember being afraid. Being allied with another human being was a terrifying idea for me then; it is only slightly less terrifying now.

I may have been in love with her, though it seems unlikely.

In any case, as I have said, we had something in common, something of great importance. I was saddened to learn of her death. When I first read the story it didn't mean anything. I may have thought to myself—'what an odd thing, someone else named Alice Turley from southern New Jersey.' But of course I knew at once who it was, and what had happened, and I also suspected that she hadn't died of 'natural causes.' Perhaps she had been following events in Phnom Penh, thinking, as I was today, of Duch, of Tuol Sleng. Perhaps not. Perhaps she had moved on, just as I had, though one never does really move on, not from war. The author of the obituary did not include every salient fact about her life. How could he have done so? That Alice was an extraordinary woman, that she learned the Khmer language out of a love for a country that most Americans couldn't locate on a map, that she worked in Cambodia during the worst days of the war and was among the last Americans to leave the capital, that she was taken prisoner by the Khmer Rouge and forced to see things that no American in Cambodia ever saw—these were facts that were omitted, and if I thought it would make a difference, I could write to the *Inquirer* and set them straight. But then, what evidence did I have of what Alice had told me that day, what proof could I offer? Better to keep quiet.

My habit, late each day, is to take a short walk in the park near my apartment. In the evenings, all year around, Albuquerque is profoundly silent, aside, of course, from the noise of traffic, but of human voices there is no evidence as everyone, it appears, is content to remain indoors. The blue lights of televisions flicker through the night like distress signals on a frozen sea. When I walk I sometimes consider the notion, absurd of course, that consciousness exists apart from reality, apart from human beings, a Hegelian *Geist* that can reflect on reality and make sense of it. The digital signals that nightly mesmerize my apartment complex—and Vista del Arroyo is, I suspect, no different from anyplace else—these electrons are the same ones that flow through the stars and through me. Perhaps 'consciousness' is a glossary that we require to make sense of one another and of the world we inhabit. And now that she is gone, what is 'Alice Nye Turley' but neurons firing in my brain? Here, nightly, freighted onto these bits of wobbling light are soothing pictures and sounds—I can only offer this as a supposition—that offer Mrs. Menendez, a fan, in particular, of the *telenovella*, respite from something that I want desperately to embrace. I don't want to rest, not yet, not until the business I have here is finished. And what is that business? I don't think that I will walk tonight.

Coincidently, I met Alice on the same day, and nearly at the same time, that the fortieth president of the United States was taking the oath of office—late in the morning of January 20, 1981. It is strange to remember something so precisely, but then I also remember what I was doing during the swearing in of Kennedy, Johnson (both times), and Obama. I was in Vietnam for the second of Nixon's inaugurations, attended Mr. Carter's with a sense of false hope, and don't recall the others. Most of us who are of a certain age can recollect what they were doing during the most dangerous days of the Cuban missile crisis, the assassination of Kennedy, the demolition of the Berlin Wall, and, of course, the moment the jetliner struck the north tower of the World Trade Center. My meeting with Alice was one of those handful of moments in life that you remember no matter what, no matter how long you live or what other experiences you have—an unforgettable moment not because of its profundity, but because the circumstances of your life, the arrangement of your emotions, the status of your consciousness, the barometric pressure—whatever—allows it to poke through the debris of banality that came before and after in just the way sumac trees push up through the cinders of railroad beds in the most blasted of landscapes. What were the circumstances of that day? What state was I in on a day that, in retrospect, changed everything for me and for the rest of us as well? I can easily find out by reading my notebooks.

I leave all the lights in the apartment off except for the light above the stove. Frank Morgan has given way to Sarah Vaughn. The room is cold so I grab a sweater. The soccer players are gone, and the park, which I can see from my living room, is empty save for a lone dog walker. This is a city where the stars are visible—not just Orion, which I recall seeing even in the smoggiest years of my residence in Philadelphia, but Cassiopeia, Urus Major, and Andromeda, constellations I learned as a child in the clear air of New Jersey. Cold, thinking air. This city was once the preferred destination of tubercular patients. In the nineteen-teen's there was a sanatorium—St. Joseph's— not far from here. "Lungers" were welcomed by some and shunned by others—there's still TB on the reservations west and north of the city. The guy upstairs, who's stomp- ing around right now, breathes with the help of a porta- ble oxygen tank, not because of tuberculosis but from a lifetime of smoking. He's a grim, overweight ex-uranium miner who is in a losing negotiation with death. He has a gun collection that fills one room of his shabby apart- ment—pistols and shotguns and a thousand-dollar AR-15 like the one I carried in Vietnam and Cambodia. Frank lets me bring him meals on Sundays, though he doesn't like me for my liberal views and "wasteful" profession. He's learned from talk radio that teachers are pinkos and queers who teach just so they can have a summer vacation. I don't argue with him—he's dying—but his bile upsets my equilibrium. We're an odd mix here on this end of the planet. Swimming in privilege, living as if history never happened. I suppose for us it never did. Mrs. Menendez doesn't speak to Señor Francis because he once called her a "wetback," which she isn't, having been born in Albuquerque of a family that lived in Nuevo Mexico three hundred years before the first O'Malley set foot on Ellis Island. But our resentments run deep and have nothing to do with what's real or unreal—"faith-based" bigotry is the way to go these days. This worries me because of what I do remember, though I'm trying to remember less, not to "dwell" as my mother once said, on those things over which I have no control. But then you hear on the radio words that bring everything back, everything terrible that has transpired during your brief life, and you see the signs of the whole damn thing beginning again.

Ta Mok was among the most murderous of the Khmer Rouge, certain of himself, ruthless with his rivals. I heard this on the radio today, or perhaps Alice told me in 1981. She met him during the time she was a captive of cadres of the Khmer Rouge in 1975. She told me how she was sent by the CIA to a village in Anlong Veng and was taken prisoner by Ta Mok's forces. The details are here, in one of the notebooks in which I recorded my conversations with Alice. The woman on the radio said today that Ta Mok had been imprisoned with Duch but had died of *natural causes* before his trial. Died of "natural causes." Perhaps he smoked himself to death. Father Ho was a chain smoker, so was Stalin. I quit years ago. Lenin was a puritan.

Every night I eat in the living room at a tray table. When I was growing up we called them TV tables, and I loved nothing more than sitting on Sunday nights—the only night it was permitted—eating in the living room, watching the *Hallmark Hall of Fame* with my family. Now, when I set my plate and wine glass down on the cheap metal table, I feel the weight of the years in a way that I don't at any other time. I ask how half a century could have passed—more—but only as a formality. One knows perfectly well how and why time passes, there's no mystery any longer; time is, in a sense, all that there is, all that remains real as we pry away the layers of pretense and illusion. Ten thousand feet above sea level tiny white and red lights blink into the dense blackness of a February night. It's Oscar Peterson time, and someone— was it Oscar himself?—is scatting behind 'Falling in Love with Love,' great title, a memorable date.

When I'm done eating I will clean up the dishes, put on Bill Evans or Hank Jones and go to my bookshelves. I will find my notebooks for January 1981—there will probably be several because that was a period in my life when I wrote a great deal. When I find the books, I will read about Alice. The preferred phrase is "celebrate:" I will celebrate the life of a distant comrade, someone whose solitude crossed my own, briefly, a lifetime ago.

It transpires that there are three notebooks from January 1981. Also a long letter from Alice—twenty-two densely packed pages—I'd forgotten I had it. It's a loss that we no longer write letters but send one-line emails. One notebook contains translations from German and Italian, languages I was interested in at the time, for reasons that I no longer recall. The other two notebooks are germane to the question at hand. They record the events of the days that led up to the 20th in remarkable detail. They address the question. And what is that question? I have no idea. I hardly recognize my voice, which is of course the point of writing things down—to see how far we've come.

In the pages that follow, using my notebooks, I will reconstruct the events of the day I met Alice, what I was thinking about, our meeting, our conversations, and everything I can remember of what she told me of her life. I will edit, extrapolate, cut and paste, make some guesses but try to avoid lying. Material that I add from other notebooks or as editorial comment and clarification will be duly noted. I will record more than is needed, if only to put myself in mind of that period of my life. I have to be honest: my writing is a tangle of scrawls, odd notes, events that I cannot recognize or recall, passages from books I was reading, and some eccentricity. But I was never a crazy vet—a drug user or alcoholic. At one time I had flashbacks and PTSD—but I want to insist upon my reliability as a narrator. I will also reproduce Alice's life story from notes I took after our night together, from her letter, and from memory. My version of her obituary.

Cambodia. I did things that were part of a war that I

believed in, and then I was forced to do things that I knew were wrong. I spilled innocent blood, and if I am ever to forgive myself, it must be soon. It was Alice who showed me the way toward forgiveness.

I

January 20, 1981

It's morning, the end of January, uncommonly cold for Philadelphia, with mounds of dirty snow left over from a Christmas storm. I am working in the basement of the Van Pelt library. The light is dim here in the BRs where I spend every day. My desk is illuminated by florescent lights that sometimes flicker when the wind blows. A slice of morning sky is visible in the bunker-style window above me. The walls are raw cinder block, functional in a way that suggests mere aesthetics don't count. Cold and gray, but quiet and restful. A million books.

Each morning I leave my room a couple of miles west of the University and take the streetcar that runs east and west on Baltimore Avenue. The trolley, built in the 1920s, carries service workers, students, and laborers down the iron tracks to Center City. Graffiti defaces the ceilings, the windows, the seats—black scrawls denoting West Philly gangs, the tags running over one another, marking territory. On both sides of the Avenue there are three-decker houses, neat twins, run-down apartments, all put up after World

War II for the white workers who toiled in the insurance companies, banks, and industrial firms clustered downtown at the feet of William Penn. A decade ago, when court-ordered busing and working-class blacks threatened property values, whites headed west and north, leaving the City and its stunted sycamores and dying elms behind. The houses I stare at each morning were left to the poor people who roll in as the tide of the middle class rolls out. As whites fled to ethnic enclaves like Bala and Havertown, or went further west to college towns like Haverford and Villanova, black families, just out from under Jim Crow, tore up their roots in the red hills of Georgia and the tobacco bottomlands of the Carolinas and headed North. There was work in Philly after the war, factories on the edges of the city—you can see them now, burned out and boarded up, moved, ironically, to the South, where wages are low and unions nonexistent, soot-stained hulks whose faded signs—International Machine Tools, Northeast Packaging, Penn Meat Processing—proclaim not only the passing of companies and jobs and lives, but the death of industry. Nobody has bothered to tear the buildings down. They stand surrounded by burdock and soap week, clots of stunted grass and fields of cinders, next to the Amtrak station and the rusted rails of the Great Northern, all with the stolid look of those bombed-out European cities you saw in newsreels after the War. All of us here in Philly are waiting for someone to raise us from the dead—to raise the City itself up from the dead—but no one is coming, and the ghosts who ride the trolley understand.

White ethnics, Center City Wasps, black sons and daughters of sharecroppers, Amish-Germans, Irish and Italians,

Koreans and Vietnamese and Cambodians moving into the shops and slums that edge my neighborhood. No place on earth is closer to Bedlam. The uncollected garbage, vials of crack crushed on the sidewalks, families living in boxes, the stench of fear—the air itself thick with despair. Brotherly love having gone the way of the City Upon a Hill, we're just keeping out of one another's way.

I pulled the cord at Fifteenth and Walnut. The conductor knows me and waited a few extra beats while I eased down the stairs.

"Thanks Mel, see you later."

"Yep, see you."

I limped down the quad, past the bookstore and the high-rise dorms, the faculty club and classroom buildings.

The snow was wet and clung to my boots, and the dampness seeped into my bones.

Universities are welcoming places. The downtown public library was available to me, but I preferred the liberality and fresh air of Franklin's college, an expression of American optimism and Enlightenment.

A bitter wind blows up Locust Walk.

The regular students, just beginning to arrive from a long vacation, flow past me like bright water. They are bundled up and hustling to get indoors. Their clothes are shabby in a studied way. The boys affect disengagement, the young women, pretty in the way prep school girls tend to be, well-groomed and chic, know enough not to walk alone even here, and lean close to their friends and lovers. Violence nibbles at the edges of this serene campus. The brick walls and stately buildings are not enough to keep the city at bay. Some of the boys look at my shattered leg and nod to themselves. They know I don't belong here, but Mr. Franklin chose to put his college in the democratic center of the city, and it's too late to keep me out.

On Walnut Street, a block from the library, a line of silver food trucks is parked, each selling steaming cups of coffee, doughnuts and rolls, pretzels with mustard, Chinese food and cheese steaks. Kuo Seng, a friend of a few years, greets me, then hands me a brown sack with two cups of coffee and a couple of corn muffins. Seng and I met at a hockey game half a decade before. We sat together, began a conversation, and drank a beer. Later, Seng told me a little about his life—how he had escaped from Cambodia, how his mother and father disappeared into the jungles near Batdambang, and how his brother, taken by communist cadres in April 1976, was never heard from again. Seng escaped into Thailand, immigrated to Canada, and obtained a visa to work in the United States. He'd lived in Boston and Brooklyn, worked in construction, and taught Khmer for the Cherry Street Quaker Meeting. He worked hard for five years, lived in a house with a dozen other Cambodians, spent little, and purchased a food truck. He's married now, owns a flat in West Philly, and is getting rich.

I practiced my Khmer on him: "*Niak sohk sabaay te?*"

"Forget it. Speak English.."

"Sorry. What's good today?"

"There will be dumplings for lunch—*shuijiao*, steamed," Han said.

"And your wife?"

"The sweetest blossoms bloom in the evening," he said in Khmer. I understood every word.

—⁓—

[Inauguration Day]: James Earl Carter was a peanut farmer and nuclear engineer from Plains, Georgia. Ronald 'Dutch' Reagan was born in Tampico, Illinois. Both men had been governors and both presented themselves, with, I believe, unequal disingenuousness, as outsiders in politics. Carter was Born Again; Reagan's beliefs are obscure. He's a chameleon—an FDR Democrat transformed into a Barry Goldwater Republican—how does that happen? Both men are ambitious, but their ambitions have led them to adopt different public faces: Carter's has been sanctimonious; Reagan is the cover boy for the ingenuous. Reagan won the election handily.

When I was born Harry S Truman was president. He had been a haberdasher. The 'S' didn't stand for anything. He seemed honest, but now I have my doubts.

Mr. Carter failed to rescue the hostages from Teheran and collapsed while running. He was accused of being 'weak' and therefore lost the election to Mr. Reagan who is 'strong.' Americans prefer 'strong' leaders who pledge to 'get things done.' What they do is often a matter of indifference.

Since I don't read newspapers and don't own a TV I'm unsure of my ground here. The other day, riding into Penn on the trolley, a black woman who was flipping through the *Daily News* clicked her tongue and said to no one in particular 'looks like another war.' All that day those words kept me off balance. She was referring, I suppose, to Nicaragua.

On Bedlam: Louis Agassiz, professor of zoology at Harvard, wrote in 1863, "No efforts should be spared to check that which is abhorrent to our better nature, and to the progress of the higher civilization and a purer morality . . . Conceive for a moment the difference it would make in future ages, for the prospect of republican institutions and our civilization generally, if instead of the manly population descended from cognate nations the United States should hereafter be inhabited by the effeminate progeny of mixed races, half Indian, half negro, sprinkled with white blood—I shudder from the consequences."

And then there is the imprecision of the words that fill the pages of the books in the Van Pelt. For example, the last book I held yesterday was Robert Burton's *Anatomy of Melancholy*, and the final words of my day, written out in this notebook, were from section one, partition two, page 5 of the VP's lovely eighteenth century edition, where Burton offers that inveterate melancholy may be cured *nil desperandum*—whatever that means—it is upon this good hope that we proceed. Burton, one of my principal authorities, is also excellent on libraries, on sitting, on bile, on apoplexy. What if all of these volumes that surround me contain nothing true, but represent a great conspiracy, not a lie, but nothing at all, an emptiness? Or if they are a labyrinth leading nowhere, or to madness?

"Nobody really understands the human condition unless he realizes that apart from one or two persons, there is not one soul who is interested in whether he lives or dies." Henry de Montherland, an author new to me, believed this to be true, but it is unbearable to think so. I found this sad thought by accident, while looking for something else—I forget what it was—and copied the unwanted idea in my notebook so that it wouldn't haunt my memories. The things I write down I'm allowed to forget, but everything else remains available, right there, in the bright light of consciousness.

—⁓—

He was overcome with great compassion and uttered this in sadness: Krpaya paraya visto/visidann idam abravit/drstve'mam svajanam krsna/yuyutsam samupasthitam. Arjuna, the human hero of the *Bhagavad-Gita*, utters these words in the first book, line 28, as he looks out at his kinsmen, arrayed for a great battle—the Kurus—but also his kinsmen's enemies: *My limbs shake, my mouth is dry, my body shakes, my hair stands on end.* Arjuna protests to the god Krishna that he doesn't wish to kill anyone—his kinsmen in particular. He doesn't wish to fight. *My skin burns; I cannot stand; my mind reels.* The piling together of details clinches the mood; the hero will have to be persuaded to take up Gandiva, his mythic bow. Only by being persuaded that the world is illusion, that death is not an end to life but a portal to Being and, most horribly, in being told that he must kill because it is his duty to kill, does Arjuna relent—and he kills.

When Arjuna wishes to look on Krishna's divine form, the god gives him a new set of eyes. Like a burning bush, or a voice from heaven, decaying scrolls stuffed in jars and hidden in caves: the mystery of the world is hidden in plain sight. So Arjuna sees the universe in great flashes—the music in the background a *raga* or *Rite of Spring*, Krishna a rainbow of light and Arjuna dazzled.

⁓

"It seems not to be the case that there is a Power in the universe which watches over the well-being of individuals with parental care and brings all their affairs to a happy ending." Lovely understatement! Only Freud, the least ironic of thinkers, could compose such a bloodless and yet passionate sentence.

⁓

There are ten names that must not be erased. Today is Tuesday, so as soon as the doors were opened and I said good morning to John, I went down to my carrel, placing my bag with coffee and corn muffins on the desk—against the rules, but the librarians look the other way. I walked down one flight to the BDs, into the entrails of theology, philosophy, patristics and apologetics, over one range, and then to the bottom shelf on the right by the exit door, to Gershom Scholem's books on Kabala. Scholem is someone I read regularly. He had been in school with Walter Benjamin in Germany. When Hitler came to power Scholem had urged his friend to get out, to go to Palestine before it was too late, but Benjamin didn't listen, he was too deeply engaged in his Arcades project, his archaeology of the nineteenth century, unwilling to leave home—though he had no home, he stayed with women who loved and pitied him, who respected his intellect—he stayed too long, tried to escape, crossed the Pyrenees, hid briefly in Spain, but, rather than fall into the hands of the Gestapo, took an overdose of morphine in Port-Bou.

On page 533 of my copy of Benjamin's *Arcades Project*, in the discussion of Panoramas, he writes of Lemercier's *Lampelie et Daguerre*, that the latter "made a radiant theatre of optics" transcending both the stationary and flat panoramas whose triumph came in '*Le Tour du Monde*,' a miraculous replica of the known world exhibited at the Paris World exhibit of 1900, by turning a bare cloth into "a mirror of nature itself." Daguerre, whose own dioramas evoked, among other historical scenes, the revolutionary world of Paris in 1830, charmed Balzac, who claimed to have anticipated the daguerreotype in **Louis Lambert**. Balzac, whom Benjamin admired for, among other things, creating a sequence of stories in which no fewer than five hundred minor characters play virtually no role—*five hundred!*—making Dickens look slothful by comparison. The Van Pelt is an Arcade. It is my nineteenth century—the unrecoverable past.

With Scholem, I enter the ghostly realm. Think of it. All the spirits of history are here. All of the dead.

God is thought, not volition. Emanations of God are found in the secrets of ideas. But the ordinary mind isn't up to the task of finding the One. The mind must be prepared. The cloak of the body must be set aside through deep esoteric learning. The Thought that thinks Itself. But the mind comes quickly upon *afisah*—nothingness. We must be prepared to step into nothingness ourselves: we are immersed in **the nothing that is God**. How better to know the divine but negatively, by knowing what He is not. The world is **thought** transformed into being. No, not that, the truth is harder: the world is the nothingness of God. Wittgenstein wrote in regard to the *Tractatus* that his ethical theories could not be spoken about—they existed in the silence beyond language. He told a would-be publisher that readers might understand the deeper ideas contained in the slender book by imagining what was *not* written in it.

The meaning of emptiness can be whatever we wish it to be. And if our wishes are benign, then the silence of the universe, the white spaces in books, the words left unspoken, all of these things might be filled with joy. But sometimes silence is just that.

The patron saint of libraries is Gabriel Naudé who brought order to the greatest library of the seventeenth century, the Bibliothèque Mazarine—great in its breath and scope and the bravery of its collections. Naudé's *Advis pour dresser une bibliotheque*, published in 1644, was the first description of the kind of universal repository of learning enshrined in the *ficciones* of Jorge Luis Borges. All of learning is to be encompassed in the universal library, all authors, ancient and modern, in their original languages and in the most deluxe editions. Other admirable collections, in the view of Naudé, were the Bodleian, the Ambrosiana, the Bibliothèque du Roy in Paris—all of which I visited at one time—also the Vatican—which I have seen only from the Great Foyer—the Marciana in Venice, the library of Cambridge University, and, closer to home, the sub-basements of the Widener Library at Harvard where, with forged academic credentials, I was able to spend three weeks reading the papers of William

James before being removed by campus security. Of the institutions of culture, I have preferred libraries, for their memories, their utility, their pretensions toward universality, their dusty quiet.

—∿∿—

"I spend there most of the days of my life and most of the hours of the day; I am never there at night," wrote Montaigne of his library, the third floor of a tower on the Chateau de Montaigne. "In calm and freedom from all cares he will spend what little remains of his life." I walked the grounds of the Chateau in 1977, sipping from a wineskin. In the Bodleian, later that same year, I examined the single surviving manuscript of *Beowulf*, preserved in the library of Sir Robert Cotton; the stained letters of Old English, run on and unpunctuated, were difficult to make out, but not much more so than the handwriting of Dante Rossetti or Thomas Carlyle. I also stared at the letters of Coleridge and Wordsworth, of George Eliot to her husband, of G.B. Shaw and Virginia Woolf ("Oh that our human pain could here have ending"). Reeling from hours spent staring into glass cases, I left the building and walked in a rainstorm to the closest pub. Already drunk, I sobered up on tea and cheese sandwiches before going back for more. "Entering a library, I am always struck by the way in which a certain vision of the world is imposed upon the reader through its categories and its order," writes Alberto Manguel. The world of the VP is subdued, subterranean, stiff and rigorous, utilitarian—steel shelves packed in long rows, spare illumination, uncarpeted floor, raw cement walls—hospitable and quiet, often, as now, deserted.

In his treatise *The Compound of Alchymie*, written in 1471, George Ripley, Canon of Bridlington in Yorkshire, describes calcination, the first step on the road to the transmutation of elements, as the turning of earth into water, of water into air, of air into fire and fire back into earth. The result of this long process is the production of the ashes of Hermes' trees—the natural, irreducible stuff of which all life is composed. The idea of rendering one thing into another is the goal of all art, of all thought, of each life. At the end, the quintessence of our humanity—our redemption.

"In today's world, personal truth is the only reality. To stand by that truth–to declare it–is revolutionary." The writer Hans Erich Nossack, who died just a few years ago, nearly unknown in America, wrote in *Untergang*, his eye-witness account of the firebombing of Hamburg, his city, "Now time sits down sadly in a corner and feels useless." It was in Guernica, in 1939, that airplanes first dropped bombs on civilians with the purpose of terrorizing—and, of course, killing them. In Hamburg, between visits to libraries, I went to a gallery to look at the photographs of Erich Andres. One photo shows twisted corpses turned to charcoal by the fires ignited by incendiary bombs—an image that is difficult to look at, pornographic in its depiction of violated human bodies. Another shows the skeleton of a building that reminds me each time I see it of Ground Zero in Hiroshima. The one I now remember as I browse among the hopeful words of theologians and philos-ophers (the faint gray light barely penetrates these ranges; I leave the overhead lights off) show living men and women

making their way through a rubble-strewn street amid dusty, diffused light. Two men carry bicycles on their backs—there is no question of their being able to ride through the chunks of stone and mortar—while an old woman, whose stripped dress looks like the forlorn clothing of the condemned at Birkenau, carefully negotiates the broken street. The line of people stretches into the vanishing point at the center of the photograph, which was then hanging on a wall on a side street of Hamburg, a street similar to the one in the photo, narrow, rebuilt of course, packed with shops and cafés and pedestrians. I asked the owner of the gallery, a thick, florid man whose beard was a shade of white I had never seen before, as white as a cooked egg, if his shop were on the street captured by Andres's photograph, the one that had riveted me for a quarter of an hour, whose texture was as flat and bland as those haunting photographs of the dead that had just begun to arrive from Cambodia, from the "killing fields" as they are being called. I spoke German poorly, though it was a language I had heard growing up, German filling the rooms of our apartments as aunts and uncles newly arrived from the old country, the old disgraced country, passed through on their way to new lives, lives, perhaps, of equal disgrace. German is a language I love to read but despair of speaking—back then, not cogent in any case, I choked on the words as I addressed the egg-faced man, and he looked at me with amusement, perhaps disdain, and said that no, that we were standing in an entirely new and rebuilt part of the city, one that had not been in the quarters that were destroyed, and that if I wished to visit the older parts of town I could take the tram or a cab—he pointed to the door to indicate the direction in which one might find the remainder of the world. I took the hint and left, but I had no real interest in locating the scene of the photograph that had so arrested me in the gallery; the effect was felt and registered, the truth of the image burned, as it turned out, forever into my memory. Now in whatever city I find myself, as I walk the streets, it is easy to imagine the graceful brick apartments and shops lying cracked in the dusty air, the hurrying pedestrians moving like ghosts through the streets they grew up in, wondering how they would eat or where they might sleep.

It hardly takes bombs to destroy what is so painfully constructed. This isn't the picture, but it is one not unlike it that I have cut from a magazine and have placed in this notebook, on this winter day, 20 January 1981. In the future, I wonder if I will remember this moment of preserving the image, the recollection, the event itself. So many layers of time dropped upon one another like pamphlets warning those below of what is to come.

The Romantics enjoyed visiting ruins. Creating them as well. The mossy scattered granite shards of a Roman temple or a defensive wall in York—such as that described by Bede in his *History of the English Church and People*—embodiments of the sublime—attracted parsons and poets—Wordsworth made the Grand Tour on foot, the poor man's tour, in 1790, with his undergraduate friend Robert Jones, skirting Paris to avoid the crowds of *fédérés* celebrating the fall of the monarchy—the vivacious Elizabeth Bentley, whose survey of the Lake Country—she had recently broken with the proud Mr. Darcy, nothing was better than ruins for a broken English heart—revived her spirits for the romantic skirmishes to come. Henry James, a curious but by no means eager traveler who ambled among ruins to gird his imagination for his great female characters, or the writers who rambled from Rye to Sandhurst, from the small farmhouse lent by Ford Maddox Hueffer to his admired Polish friend Jozef Teodor Konrad Korzeniowski; Stevenson and Southey, Miss Eliot and Miss Woolf, inspected the remnants of the murky English past flung across the damp Cotswold's and Midlands, the Lakes and the promontories of the Scottish Highlands. Broken stones and shards of the past put the poet in the proper frame of mind to mediate upon his own past—ruins reminded Wordsworth of the sublime moments of his childhood, of great friendships and lost loves.

—ᨆ—

[2012]: My grandmother, Gertrude Bushmüller, an unassuming woman with thin white hair, a chain smoker who drank thirty cups of sweet tea each day, who worked in hot kitchens until she was seventy-five while her husband, Frederick, my grandfather, a mechanic, a man who could fix anything that was broken and break anything that was whole, labored for the Penn Central Railroad, Jay Gould's great octopus, though by the 1950s it was a ruined enterprise, bankrupted several times over by the great robber baron and his successors. My grandparents and my mother lived in Bethlehem, Pennsylvania, a town of soot-cloaked houses tethered to one another like the drab lines of men with lunch pails who stood for the Factory Street bus in the January cold. Germans mostly, like my family, also some Irish, Ukrainians and Lithuanians, Catholics one and all, not poor, the hard-working lower middle classes, 'ethnics', union men, a few socialists and communists, men with rough hands who built things and tended to their families; women with thick legs and joyless lives—childbearing, work, intemperate husbands, men like my grandfather, who overcame war and emigration to start over, not asking for much, grateful to be alive and in a place that was unlikely to be interested in his past. When I was in my twenties and visited the town, when I drove past my grandmother's house, a green asbestos-sided wreck on Methuen Street, in the midst of a slanting, narrow enclave a block from the steel mill, treeless but for a few half-dead elms, a street where kids played stickball in dusty yards, where the unemployed sat on the hoods of worked-over Chevys and drank tallboys or wine out of paper sacks, I noted that the family mansion had become home to a black family that had probably moved up from the Southside. The Bushmüllers, later the Bushes, moved out of the neighborhood when they'd scrapped together a few dollars and a generation of respectability. The black family might do the same, but it was less likely. My grandparents didn't move far—to Philly's Northeast, and then to the Jersey Shore—paradise in those days—and that's where their journey ended.

—◈—

[January 20, 1981]: Daydreaming for nearly an hour—my coffee grown cold—and jotting these notes, and now back to reading Scholem's description of the *Heikhalot*, the seven palaces in the celestial Garden of Eden. The Book of Concealment. The Secrets of the Book. I let myself fall into the words and into the half imaginable images of heaven and hell. Isaac the Blind. Nathan of Gaza. Nehemiah Hayon. Isaac Luria. I read now that Luria spent seven years in seclusion on an island near Cairo where he studied the Zohar. What did he dream of? I close my eyes and see him in his brown woolen robes, closed up in his study, dim light and a handful of books—thick parchment and faded ink. (It is as quiet here on this January day as in a monastic cell.)

The Greeks and the Hebrews heard voices and had visions—dreams. Where did these voices and images originate? And language, the Babel of tongues, presented confusions as well: where do these sounds come from? Marks on paper that transmit thoughts and feelings. The gods might be responsible, speaking to us while we sleep, uttering thoughts in a form we can understand, in a form that elicits behaviors. Isaac Luria *felt* the symbolic world and preserved it in Hebrew words (later Arabic and Spanish and Latin): the void within filled up with sound, and this was a source of wonder.

I've read about Bode's Law, the hypothesis that the planets lie at proportionate distances from the sun. The Cabalists suspected what mathematics has proven. As a child I often was taken to the boardwalk and to the ocean that lay across the filthy, blackened sand. My mother would hold my hand and walk across the cold beach, and when we would at last reach the point where the waves broke over the land my mother would point out the air holes of the sand crabs that opened as the water rushed back into the sea. The holes would open and shut quickly, with a sputtering that seemed desperate. I imagined the tiny animals suffocating in the murky water. The ruined hulk of a freighter lay just off shore, perched on a sandbar, the shattered remains of a German U-boat, sunk by the Coast Guard in 1945, the year our neighbor Hattie Greenwald and her family were transported from the village of Piaski in eastern Poland to the ghetto at Lublin and later to Majdanek where she contracted typhus and nearly died, but as she told my mother *God saw fit to spare her* and take her mother and father and two brothers to Belzec so that she could come to live on Second Avenue and work in Ladies Garments at Steinbach's on First Avenue. Hattie Greenwald lived alone and sang softly to herself in the early morning. She took the bus downtown at seven o'clock; she was always nicely dressed and wore white gloves on the hottest days. When my mother worked at the hotel on weekends, or if she was too sick to get out of bed, Hattie, if she were free that day, would come across the hall and take care of me. She read me my favorite books, stories of cowboys and Indians, and made cups of cocoa that we drank in silence. One day she came into our apartment, dressed as if for work, and told us that she was going home. My mother said how nice, to go home, back, my mother supposed to Piaski. Mrs. Greenwald smiled at this and said in her quiet voice that she would miss us, and then she hugged us goodbye and kissed my forehead and walked out the door. I went to the window and watched her walk down the street and turn the corner onto Ocean Avenue.

SS *Obersturmführer* August Häfner, attached to *Einsatzgruppe* C near the Ukrainian town of Bjelaja Zerkow, near Kiev, testified at his trial for crimes against humanity as follows: "I went to the woods alone. The Wehrmacht had already dug a grave. The children were brought along in a tractor. The children were taken down from the tractor. They were lined up along the top of the grave and shot so they fell into it. The wailing was indescribable." Prosaic. I read these words in a German book, *Tagebücher eines Abwehroffiziers 1938-40.* I stole this book from the Strand in New York City. It was slightly worn, soiled and greasy. The words of Häfner and of others lay there on the pages among books about the American presidents, the Civil War and the bombing of Pearl Harbor. I had flipped through a book about Himmler, pausing at his school photo, marveling at the dullness of his features but wondering if it was possible to look clearly at the visage of such a monster. The certainty of their words. Plato spoke ironically through his Socrates, Aristotle was earnest but muddled; I suppose complacent confidence had come later on, after Hume and Kant, when the romantics began to dismantle thinking so as to advance the cause of the sovereign self. What did these men feel watching the children fall into the shallow grave? Häfner held the hand of "one small blond girl" just before she too was shot. After the war some of the men who were there at Bjeleja Zerkow, those who survived the Russian winter and the Red Army, took jobs in German business, were ordained as Lutheran ministers or Catholic priests, married their sweethearts (who perhaps had been raped by Russian soldiers), had families of their own. One former SS officer won the Nobel Prize. Did God look on these events with sadness or with the Sovereign Indifference born of His Divine Foreknowledge? The great writer Primo Levi, chemist and philosopher, survived Auschwitz and then, many years later, apparently threw himself down a stair-case in Turin. Did God's Adoring Angels weep for the blond girl, or for Levi, as I had in the Strand Bookstore? It was a bright, warm day, my birthday, humid in the crowded shop. There was a pretty young woman sitting on a bench near me reading a French history of Siam Reap. She noticed that my eyes were tearing and seemed about to speak to me when I said to her that it was all right, I was touched by something I had read, nothing was wrong. She smiled uneasily; no doubt I seemed odd, perhaps unbal-anced. She nodded and resumed reading her book, fixing her glasses and brushing brown hair back from her face. The gesture was touching. Women moving their hair away from their faces as they read--here is a rich subject for the student of beauty. That day I stood awkwardly with my book, wondering if I needed to purchase it, knowing that I wouldn't forget the words and that I might not have the courage to read any further. What if I had spoken to the young woman, asked her name? She may have been afraid of me, or perhaps she only spoke French, a language I cannot speak, and we would both have been embarrassed. In the end, I left the store. I walked out the door with my book, unpaid for, under my arm. Now when I see it there on the shelf I think about the dark-haired girl and the blond-haired girl together. I have allowed them to become one in my memory.

—⁄⁄⁄—

[January 20, 1981]: I have been looking at photographs in the older, bound periodicals. I came upon one quite by chance of Kurt Gödel and Albert Einstein walking on a grassy pathway at the Institute of Advanced Studies in Princeton, taken in the winter of 1953. In the photo, taken by Leonard McCombe, the sky is gray. The tall oaks are black and bare. Einstein's head is inclined slightly toward the younger man's. I can make out his long white hair, in stark contrast to the dapper fedora worn by Gödel. The brilliant young German, Einstein's favorite companion in the last years of his life, was perhaps challenging the flaws in Einstein's views of the unified field theory. In making mathematical predictions about the form, structure, beginning and ending of the universe, Einstein found the need to posit what came to be known as a cosmological constant. If the universe were to be static, it required, in Einstein's view, an additional energy density sufficient to "flatten" it, so that gravitational forces would not pull it apart. Later observations by Edwin Hubble demonstrated that the universe is expanding; Einstein's "blunder" was to fail to perceive this possibility. I am writing words that I do not fully understand, but the metaphor attracts me. Equilibrium is better than expansion or contraction. I imagine that within each of us there lies the opposed forces of gravity and levity, weightiness and lightness of being, forces that pull us toward others opposed by forces that tear us away from the center of our own being. The dark matter of the world—matter that acts on us without our knowledge—dislodges us from the path we should walk, *hokhmat ha-zeruf*, the way of righteousness in Scholem's text. For his part, Gödel was content to show that all theories are incomplete, all knowledge limited, reason a hopeful monster.

———

Near the restrooms on the first floor I can hear someone's radio tuned to the University station. As I walked into the loo, I heard the reporter say "the President-elect is shaking hands with President Carter and embracing Mrs. Carter." There was more, but I couldn't hear it.

———

Photography is an imperfect art depending as it does on the interposition of a complex technology, a technology informing the artist's eye with an image that is mediated—Plato would complain of yet another layer placed between the maker and the truth, but his complaint is no concern of mine. There are photographs that compel me in a way that the representations of life, the 'ideas' that Locke supposed stuck in our souls, never do. This one, the last in my notebook, is quite famous. This particular photograph shows train tracks in the snow, tracks whose black serpentine lines end at their vanishing point in a low-lying barracks-like building, one which I image to have been in Auschwitz or Buchenwald (it doesn't matter). The train rolls toward the building; German soldiers, *Schutzstaffel*, and camp capos wait on the platform for the train full of Polish Jews from Lublin to arrive. The men and women, the children and babies on the train are frozen—the average daytime temperature in southern Poland was minus six degrees centigrade that winter of 1944. They cannot see what is in front of them, only the weak light of dawn penetrates the car in which they have been stuffed like lumber, only the gray-white snow, unbroken by footprints or trees or animals, snow that reminds the children of the day they were taken skating for the first time and held warm chestnuts in their gloved hands.

General Curtis LeMay led the squadrons of B-29s that dropped over seventeen hundred tons of incendiary devices on Tokyo late in February, 1945. One hundred thousand Japanese died.

I visited Hiroshima for the commemoration of the destruction of that city by the first atomic bomb. I attended this event as part of a delegation of Vets sent by the Philadelphia chapter of the VFW—a "friendship mission." I had been out of the Army for a couple of years, and through a mutual friend received an invitation to join the VFW. The organization was mostly World War II vets. They felt a lack of sympathy for those who had been to Vietnam. They looked at us, with our long hair and suspect politics, as tainted by defeat. My friend recommended me as a decorated war hero, which I was not, and I joined to have a cheap place to drink. After a few months the post commander invited me to attend that summer's Hiroshima commemoration, not as an honor, but out of contempt for the idea of extending a hand to a despised enemy. Perhaps they believed that I would be taken prisoner by war-maddened Japs who had never surrendered. The head of my Post, a smirking ex-tank commander who had lost his right foot near Arnhem, patted me on the back and wished me luck. He privately conveyed to me the view that my status as a veteran of a lost war made me, in the Post's eyes, the perfect ambassador. I went, of course. Had I been invited to mush a sled of dogs to the North Pole I would have accepted. And yet the North Pole would have seemed familiar in comparison to what I witnessed in Japan.

[Added in 2012 to clarify paragraphs below]: During the war, Frank Bush, *né* Frederick Bushmüller, my grandfather, was a mechanic for the Luftwaffe. He knew

a great deal about engines of all kinds, he was person-
able and easygoing, not one to make waves or to disobey
orders, so that by the end of the war he obtained the rank
of *Oberleutant*. He was able to send money to his wife, my
grandmother, in Dresden. Gertrude hadn't worked when
she was first married—her own parents weren't well off,
but as bourgeois shopkeepers they were able to under-
write my grandmother's dowry and *hausfrau* role until
the Depression eroded their income and forced her to go
to work as a governess. My mother was born in 1924 or
1925, I'm not sure which, nor is she, as all of her parents'
papers were destroyed in the bombings. My grandmother
worked in the home of Fritz Jaeger, a colonel in the SS, for
his wife, Frieda Braumiller Jaeger, caring for the couple's
three children. *Obergruppenführer* Jaeger was in command
of *Einsatzgruppen III*, assigned to duty in the southern
Ukraine. The children were well behaved, bright and intelligent, and Frau Jaeger treated my grandmother well. My
grandmother showed me a picture of the family that she
had been given as a Christmas gift in 1940. Herr Jaeger
has close-cropped brown hair, worn like a skull-cap, and a
formal white tunic, decorated with a *Deutches Kreuz* worn on
the left pocket. He looks like a priest, his face pinched and
austere. Gertrude was well-liked by the family. My mother,
a lovely girl of nineteen or twenty, was also welcome in the
Jaeger household. The fact that my grandfather was also
in service, though employed in a mundane, non-combat
role, gave my grandparents legitimacy, extra bread, and a
comfortable life, at least up until 1945. In that year, the
city of Dresden was destroyed in a series of incendiary

bombing raids conducted by the RAF and the U.S. Army Air Force. My grandmother and her daughter, my mother, were at home when the first attacks on the center of the city took place. They were able to watch the city burn from the balcony of their small flat on *Waldstrasse*, a scene which impressed itself on my mother's mind so forcefully that, twenty years later, when I was a young man struggling with adolescence and failing in high school, she could silence my complaints by reminding me of the night she witnessed the incineration of Europe's most beautiful city and of tens of thousands of its inhabitants. No adolescent problem could stand up to the destruction of Dresden.

—The Altstadt glowed red at first and then there were bright orange and white explosions, smoke poured up through the night sky so thickly it blotted out the stars and the shape of the city. And a few moments later the heaviest explosions occurred and the landscape before us turned into flames. The city burned through the night and was still on fire in the morning. When I saw the piles of charcoal lying in the street and asked my mother what they were she glared at me and pulled me quickly through the rubble to look at the burned shell of the Jaeger's home.

[January 20, 1981]: A large goddess overlooks Dresden. She survived the bombing, I have only seen her photograph, but I can imagine what the blacked stone must look like, reaching out to gather the souls of the dead.

Goering wrote to Heydrich, on July 31, 1941, right around the time my grandmother went to work for Frau

Jaeger: "I hereby charge you with making all the necessary preparations with regard to the organizational, practical, and financial aspects for an overall solution of the Jewish question in the German sphere of influence in Europe." I knew the word even as a child—*Endlösung*. In a film that was shot at Nuremberg, Göering—with Hans Frank, the highest-ranking Nazi to be tried—plays the buffoon, mugging and twitching his thick eyebrows, waving his hands and shaking his head. He appears amused at the proceedings, and never expressed regret or admitted guilt for his crimes. He was found guilty of all charges. As a final macabre joke, Goering committed suicide the night before his death sentence was to be carried out. He had smuggled potassium cyanide capsules into his cell in jars of skin cream. He suffered, apparently, from psoriasis. His body was cremated and his ashes scattered in Munich, in the Isar River. During a brief visit to Munich, a mere thirty years after Goering wrote his preemptory letter to Heydrich, I was unable to sleep or to keep any food down. Every few hours I would have to find a toilet in which to gag up the bit of bread or coffee I had consumed, or, after I began to fast, to choke up bile, saliva and blood. The doctor whom I visited told me that I had contracted a case of *giardia* in some insalubrious city (I mentioned that I had been in Italy not long before), and he prescribed 500 mg. of antibiotics, three times a day, to kill the parasite. I did not fill the prescription, nor did I remain in Munich beyond the three days it took to examine the paintings in the *Haus der Kunst*. Within hours of arriving in Berne, my mysterious illness vanished.

⁓⁓

[Added 2012]: In Japan, I took the high-speed train from the main Tokyo Station. We traveled south to Fuji-san, the lovely snow-capped volcano near the border of Shizuoka and Yamanashi provinces. The day was foggy, and, at first, it was impossible to see the mountain's peak. The vets with me were surly and had no patience with the heat and humidity. They drank too much sake and marveled at the public displays of pornography. I had fallen in love with Japan at once and planned to stay on after the delegation had left. I wasn't sure how, but in those days I often acted impetuously. The countryside was lush green: rice grew everywhere, and fruit trees—pear and apple and quince (*cydonia oblonga,* the man in the seat next to me said, the fruit Paris had offered Aphrodite, the fruit of the Garden of the Hesperides, the fruit, he told me, offered by Eve to Adam; he laughed and went back to his book). The air was dense with moisture, but an hour after we arrived at the base of Fuji, the clouds suddenly broke free and the perfect cap of snow shone in the afternoon light like an immense diamond, broken into sharp rays by shards of black rock that jutted up from the flank of the mountain. I remember making a sketch of the scene in my notebook, the trees and people milling about the base, waiting to make the trek to the top. Tourist buses packed into the narrow parking lot, souvenir stands and places to buy fish and rice. Men and women attired for Alpine survival hustled by me as I limped up the narrow defile; some wore little oxygen tanks, others had the thick boots and the heavy packs of Everest Sherpas. Everyone was earnest. The climb was a pilgrimage and not exercise or sightseeing. I walked partway up the mountain, alone, until my leg began to ache, and stayed too long. I missed my group's departure for Hiroshima.

—⁓—

[January 20, 1981]: I put Scholem back in his accustomed spot and got to my feet. My hip ached; I used my cane to brace myself and pulled down hard on the range that held Origen and Eusebius. The former had been condemned for his belief in *apokatastasis*—all things return to knowledge of God. He castrated himself and yet still he was condemned for subordinating the Son to the Father in the Trinity. These matters must have appeared weighty—certainly the consequence for entertaining heterodox views was grave. Self-castration was not uncommon in the early Church. The genitals were Satan's tools, an impediment for men who aspired to become pure spirits. Renunciation of intercourse was directed by Paul—"be even as I am"—as a stay against the pull of the world. Women, of course, were evil: revered and reviled at the same time; lusty in their youth, unreasoning always, bent upon seduction—propagation somehow unseemly, like menstruation. Holy men lived in caves or holes dug in the sand of the Sinai. Anthony one of the first, but thousands followed him; hermits, *castrati*, madmen who memorized Scripture and never spoke to a human being. The hermits ate vermin, dreamed of intercourse and cool winds. Waking visions followed their privations, images of evil spirits, she-devils and incubi, ghastly temptations like those offered to their Master. Pachomius saw flaming bodies, offal raining down from a blackened sky, monstrous beings half human and half animal. Hermits and monks were offered kingdoms of the flesh, the world, the devil. Madness; what could come of these fervid imaginings? Self-abrogation, moral austerity, relentless punishment of the sinful. The history of the West.

⁓⁓⁓

I am outside, smoking. The clouds have thickened. It will snow today, perhaps a great deal. This is of no consequence to me, as long as the library doesn't close. It must be cold in Washington.

⁓⁓⁓

Aristotle's methodical sorting (as if he'd packed his belongings away and found one odd tunic lying out—*feeling*). It occurred to me as I puffed my cigarette that history *is* affection, pathos, affliction: what's left behind once the world has been tidied up and then blown apart by reason. There are, according to Aristotle's *Categories*, ten ways in which a subject may be described. They are substance (*ousia*), quantity, quality, relations, place, time, position, state, action, affection. The Stoics reduced the list to subject, quality, state, and relation. The world is what I glimpse out of the window. Its substance is material, but I know about this in the crudest and most approximate way. Quantity is the measure of what can be perceived; my frame of reference now is minute, but imagination expands the knowable world beyond the bounds of sense. The quality of the world was dialectic in Aristotle's view. Being and Becoming, or Static and Dynamic, gray and still, cold and empty, quiet and resigned—we may imagine long strings of opposites that will place us in relation to the world, and yet we are often mistaken about what we see and describe. Our descriptions,

62

no matter how thorough, how well organized, no matter
how many categories and arrangements we employ, seem
hopelessly wrong, as if there were form and movement just
outside our range of perception. The position, state, and
action of the world, its place and time, seem redundant, and
I can feel again how overly analyzed Aristotle's version of
things became as he pared away at them with the knife of
his reason. His *affection* stops me cold. *Pathos*. Also *apathia*,
or unnatural, violent feeling; also *hedone* describing the state
of taking pleasure or pain in our own, or someone else's
affections; *ergon*, describing an affective state that is passive,
though not contemplative. Pathos, remarkably, is the Greek
word both for experience and suffering, as I learned when I
read Aeschylus's *Agamemnon* and witnessed instructive terror
of the kind that rends the flesh but refreshes the mind. Has
anyone noticed how *affection* slips into *affliction* with only a
small liquid (from a fricative to a barely noticeable curling of
the tongue toward the lower incisors)?

When I finished my smoke I walked back down into
the stacks until I came to the heavy dusty volumes of Abby
Migne's *Patrologia Latina*, Augustine's *De magistro*. I translated as I read the words that I knew well, *"There is no other
reason for the use of words than either to teach or to call something
to mind . . . when we pray there is no need of speech . . . . Though
we utter no sound, we still use words in thinking and therefore
use speech within our minds. But such speech is nothing but a
calling to remembrance of the realities of which the words are but
the signs, for the memory, which retains the words and examines
them, causes the realities to come to mind."*

I was interested in this "speech within our minds." Why should it be the case that our thoughts required words and were not formed in some other way—directly, without the intermediary of speech? And what is remembering? Was this inner language our true self, our soul as Kant apparently thought? Do we all feel the same way inside, and can we know if we do? What did my grandfather think about on that first day in Florida—how did the world look to him, and what sentences did he make up to describe his feelings? How did he convince himself to forget what he had seen and done during the war? And why should it seem so important for me to know this so many years later—no sense can be retrieved from his past, or from my own, without sorting out the 'calling to remembrance of the realities of which the words are but the signs.' The problem of philosophy can be reduced to one: how must we live? Or why should we, if we prefer the superlative. But no one thinks about such things. What we wonder about is whether the water will be warm or cold, or if the tide is going in or out, or if the undertow on the beach would prove fatal.

Goebbels, Hitler's most fervent admirer, his uncritical ear and mouth, met with 'his' Fuehrer in the spring of 1941 to discuss what would occur in the occupied zones of the Soviet Union. Operation Fritz had been renamed Barbarossa in honor of Germany's medieval warrior-king, the first of the Hohenstaufen dynasty, a madman who drowned in the Saleph River attempting to overrun Asia. After the meeting Goebbels noted in his diary "We have so much to account for that we must win, otherwise our whole people, and we ourselves, and all we love—would be erased (*ausradiert würde*)." There would be no turning back.

———

[Added in 2012]: I was shot in the leg at Firebase Charlie, in the Republic of Cambodia, on April 29, 1971.

———

[2011]: My father worked for an insurance company—he was an underwriter, meaning that he figured out ways to make money from the premiums deposited with the company while keeping enough cash on hand to pay claims. When I think of him I cannot help but think of Kafka. He was seldom at home. His work required a great deal of travel, a closet of smart suits, hand-tailored shirts, numerous bottles of after-shave. We would toss a football in the autumn, on clear cool Saturdays, before he went to the office. He would fold his suit jacket nearly over the rail of the porch at the boarding house where my mother and sister and I spent the week, and then he would roll up his monogrammed sleeves and take the football from my small hands. He kept his hat on at all times, as gentlemen did in those days, and told me to run toward the street. I often dropped his passes. He could throw a tight and unforgiving spiral, something he learned to do in high school where, he said, he was the starting quarterback of a state championship team. Later I made inquiries and found that he had dropped out of Asbury Park High School without a degree in his senior year; he had never played football or anything else. I dislike sports and fine suits, but adored my father's lies. He was the artist of the family, the one who could adjust even the smallest details of life to make things bearable.

—⁓—

[2012]: On the morning of the day that I was shot, an acquaintance of mine was telling me a story. I couldn't say if it is true or not. I reproduce it approximately as he told it. It's a story about luck. Oddly, for all of the things I have forgotten, I have remembered this story, as if I were charged by fate with doing so. This story has bearing on this narrative, hence its inclusion here.

Me and my Lurp team did a drop across the border. We were deep into no man's land. Six of us, moving through the jungle, gathering intel on NVA movements, so we drop in to pick up a prisoner, do recon. Bad luck. We step into a shitstorm, ambushed by a company-sized unit, nobody's hit, but we're pinned down pretty good, they're thumping us, automatic fire coming in close. Sergeant has us covering and ducking back, scrambling low in the underbrush so's we can make a run for it; ain't no fucking way to sit tight they'd cut us to pieces. I'm the last to go out, just face down in the mud, firing like crazy, just rocking and rolling so the others can get back, maybe make a run, but worried that they're flanking me, that they're gonna bust in on me, or get lucky with a 79. I'm lying there and the clip's done, so I'm about to reload, when damned if the firing doesn't stop. It's dead quiet. I wait a beat, reload, and then listen. Not a goddamned thing. I think oh shit they're on me but no nothing's moving. Then I hear the damndest thing—a goddamned roar, like thunder, like ground rattling, just ahead or just behind me, so loud that I couldn't tell where the sound was coming from—overhead, under me. The

66

ground's shaking. I'm like what the fuck, and then I see what's up–it's elephants, it's a fucking herd of elephants. I been in country for two tours and never seen an elephant before, and here I am in the middle of a firefight and there are twenty at least. And the gooks are gone, maybe fucking trampled so I get up and get my ass in gear, back to my boys who're hunkered down two clicks east, and they're thinking I'm dead and then I tell them, elephants up there, roaring like crazy, must of run off the NVA, or spooked 'em. And they're like, yeah fuck you, elephants. Ain't no elephants nowhere round here, stoned is what you are. So how come I'm here and not dead? Nobody's got an answer for that except you're lucky or we're lucky, so let's split this scene and so we did. I'm not shitting you man, I saw Cambodian elephants.

That was the story.

Is the story true? Are there elephants in Cambodia? Never saw one myself, but that doesn't mean anything. I wish I knew. The guy was lucky. There's no better illustration of the meaning of the word.

Later that day I was waiting in line for chow and a sniper shot me in the upper thigh, just below the hip. The round—.56 caliber from a Russian Tokarev SVT-40—I've used one myself—glanced off the bone, and the exit wound, four centimeters wide, now like a grotesque mouth gaping from the side of my leg, was sewn up in a field hospital in Saigon.

You see? Chance governs most things—my getting wounded, the elephants of Cambodia, my being here and not anyplace else—and yet free will is an appealing presumption, that we are here not by chance, but embedded in a law-governed universe that moves toward resolution, and moves us toward insight, compassion, virtuous conduct, *toward life*, toward enhanced existence. Nietzsche wrote "That no one *gives* a human being his qualities—not God, not society, not his parents, or his ancestors, not *he himself.* One is a piece of fate, one belongs to the whole, one *is* in the whole. Nothing exists apart from the whole!"

When the round hit me I didn't yell out, but fell at once to the ground, in pain and incipient shock. The sniper was at least five hundred meters away—it was a fine shot—and I guessed that he had missed my head or heart because I moved, or because he did. Those standing in line around me did not realize what had happened.

Another member of my company, a black kid from Georgia, was shot in the head and died instantly.

⸺⁓⸺

[January 20, 1981]: I have finished my cold coffee and had another smoke down underneath the stairwell. No one is around—winter term hasn't begun so the Van Pelt is empty, just a few grad students and me.

⸺⁓⸺

Sie hindern mich nicht. Sie lassen mich gehn. Rilke, his mind unbalanced by his hopeless love for Lou Salome, a woman who collected men, as men have often collected women. Freud didn't care for Rilke, or perhaps it was the other way around. Freud and Rilke and Lou took a walk together— diarists all, we have some details—and Rilke came once to Freud in Vienna. And then they never met again. Freud discovered personal life, the true self. Nothing is ever lost. If we look *carefully* within—well, no one can—but if we try, then every secret is revealed. Meaning: we can know ourselves. But so what? It isn't the ephemeral self that matters; it's the taproot of human existence that Freud unearthed, the part of us that connects our life to what is unchanging, or changes so slowly as to seem unchanging.

The Library is the only place to look for hints of this excavated core of our selves. Everything is here, someplace. I am looking for the code hidden in these books. Not mine alone. Mine is only one single letter in a chain of meaning, the long chain of the phenotype of humanity.

Religious people often speak of sin as if it were something that happens to us rather than something we choose. I believe in evil. In Vietnam we would lay at night in our holes, deep holes we dug with zest, holes in which we hid and shit and smoked and slept. And sometimes at night the moon illuminated our holes with a clean white light as if a space had opened in the night sky and allowed a half-circle of heaven to intrude on our sorry redoubt of mud and fear. And you could lie in the bottom of your personal hole and think about the night and what lay just down the hill in the dense black jungle. It was other men. But being afraid made the men become greater than they were—they were like giants, evil creatures who would emerge from the night to destroy us. That was what evil was. But it's not. The evil was why we were there in those holes to begin with and why I no longer can bear to look at the moon. ….

[2012]: At this point there are three or four pages missing from the January 20th notes. Some of what I reproduced above was guesswork—I was obviously writing quickly, as if under a spell. Tucked into the notebook that I am now holding are half a dozen sheets of paper torn from another book, undated. These pages were typed on my old Remington portable. Here's a portion of what I wrote, probably sometime before January 20th. I think they have bearing on the subject at hand.

From *Siddhartha: "It seemed to him that whoever understood this river and its secrets, would understand much more, many secrets, all secrets."*

And I wrote: *It is impossible for me to understand these insipid literary passions of mine.*

And then: *The yearning to find meaning in nature: to assume the source of life conveys its essence. A mistake. The Bodhi taught Buddha nothing; he looked within. Puerile to turn Buddhist thought toward psychological ends—Siddhartha an egotist, European to the core, clothed, he might sip aperitifs with Sartre, that fraud. Hesse though a great writer, and must be forgiven for trying his hand at Orientalism.*

And then this passage:

What do I know of Buddhism? Then again, I am now certain that a river is only a river, water flowing according to the laws of fluid dynamics, making the contours of the land and following them, breaking up the earth and at times overwhelming it, moving with what we have often been pleased to see as fatal inexorability to the sea. What are the secrets of rivers or mountains? No one could seriously believe that staring day after day at a river would make you wise. Rather, it would make you mad, or indifferent. The relief though of placing oneself outside the follies of men and women might be tempting, but outside of mystical novels such a thing is impossible.

Here's the story I typed out sometime in January 1981:

The day I read that sentence in Hesse I was in the third-class compartment of a train, fleeing Arles, a small ugly town, full of Roman ruins. I had traveled there to look at the landscape that had moved Van Gogh. I was obsessed with his pictures and traveled all over Europe to find each one and to study it and to write down in my notebooks what I saw in them. In cafés in Amsterdam and Paris and Frankfort and Munich and Arles I read the correspondence between Van Gogh and his brother Theo. It was Theo in whom I was first interested—the brother who was in love with what genius could accomplish.

My hotel room in Arles was high above narrow streets through which cars and motorbikes roared; the room was tiny, hot and stuffy, with a thin mattress and yellow sheets, stinking pits for toilets, cold-water showers. I had little money. A small disability from the Army, some savings. My diet that summer was bread and cheese and wine. My bowels were frozen shut. The air was dry and dusty in that strange city of Cathar memories—at Beziers five thousand heretics—men, women, and children—had been dragged from the Church of St. Mary Magdalene and slaughtered: "Kill them all: *Novit enim Dominus qui sunt eius.*" The God of love will know his saints. I thought of the burning churches and the children full of arrows. I read the French history of the Cathars in my room—all night I would lay awake and read—Antonin Gadal, Christianity of the Mysteries, and Hans Jonas's book on the Gnostics, a book I had purchased in Paris. Strange books, with their seeing through the world and into the light they presumed filled earthly matter. Innocent III rejoiced at the massacres. God's mercy only extends to his saints. Of this the Pope was quite certain: "By this present apostolic writing we give you Bishops a strict command that, by whatever means necessary, destroy all these heresies and expel from your lands those who hold them." Arles seemed like an unlikely place to subdue the flesh. Through the dust the sunlight danced in the trees and along the river. Here was the place Vincent had set his easel to paint the "Vineyard", the "Yellow House", "Sunflowers." I took a glass of absinthe at the Café de la Gare and reread the letters that had so touched me when I first saw them in the hospital at Ft. Dix. A lovely middle-aged woman, a widow, who volunteered with the USO, had put the book in my hand. "I want to work, I absolutely need it." This wanting to work, the heart of Vincent's complaints, the compulsion in the paintings themselves, the wild colors and thick impasto, as if the vines could be lifted from the canvas in their late summer richness, their deep scarlet—I saw them, walking for hours on the road to Fourques or to Saint-Gilles, towns that had no interest for me, the cafés seeming no different than the diners at home, the streets full of shops that held objects I couldn't recognize. But Arles was where Vincent had quarreled with Gauguin, where they had argued about painting and the look of light, about money and God.

One night in August I was sitting in a café writing in my notebook when an older man, frail, dark-skinned, asked me, in crisp English, if I were an American. I had to admit that I was, though just then, there, in that year, I would have preferred to pass for something else—Canadian perhaps—but my face, my unkempt hair and beard, the battered clothing I wore, gave me away.

The gentleman, well-dressed, graying, with a neatly-trimmed beard and mustache, asked me if I would mind if he joined me.

"Not at all." I would have preferred to remain alone, but I don't like being impolite.

The man ordered a glass of wine. He lit a cigarette and offered me one. I asked him if he were from Arles, he said yes, he lived here, and I asked if he was born here.

"No. I am Armenian. From Istanbul. I came to France many years ago."

"English is your third language?"

"No, it is my fifth. I grew up in a small community speaking Armenian, but in school we learned Turkish. When I left Turkey, when I had to leave, I passed through Italy before coming here. I'm afraid that my Italian is no longer serviceable."

I drank my coffee. He sipped his wine. We smoked and looked around at the other patrons, at the people passing in the street. The light was softening, the air cooler and lighter on one's skin. I glanced at the newspaper, then back at my companion. He smiled at me and asked my name. He reached out his hand and said that he was Nadiryan; he spoke his last name, but I didn't catch it. Since he had given me a cigarette it seemed courteous to sit with him a bit longer.

"I left Turkey because of persecution. You know of this?"

I said that I did.

"The French took me in after the war. There were many Armenians who fled Turkey, though many were not so lucky. I feel as if I've always lived here. I think in French and dream in Turkish, I write my poems in French but they feel to me like the words of another man. It is a strange thing to have traveled so far, to belong and yet to feel temporary wherever one lives—to be rootless, like so many others."

I said that I understood, though I had no experience of exile myself.

"Have you been in the war?" Nadiryan asked.

I said that I had, but in such a way as to suggest my unwillingness to speak of it.

"Yes, I thought so when I saw you. That, or you had run from it."

No, I hadn't run.

"I too was in a war," Nadiryan said. "The Turks used the coming of the war in Europe to finish what they had begun. My older brother was a newspaper reporter in the capital, a reporter for *Jamanak*, he wrote news of society, of arts and music, books. And he was taken away. Mehmet Şükrü—do you know him?— continued the persecution of the Armenian people. My family was forced to move to Istanbul in 1934. Like many thousands of others, we tried to become Turkish. But we could not. My family sent me abroad, to Italy, and I have never been back. My parents are dead. My sister lives in Sarajevo. And I am here."

And what do you do?

"I am a writer, like my brother. A poet and playwright."

Naturally I asked to read some of his work—it was the polite thing to do.

"You have been to a university?"

"Only briefly. I'm self-taught. In other words, untaught."

"Unschooled but not illiterate. I'm impressed."

"I took up books as an escape, and then pursued them for pragmatic reasons, for purposes other than learning."

"What other purpose is there?"

"For problem solving."

We smoked and talked for several hours. He shook his head, laughed at me, and offered that my tastes were those of an old man, a conservative, he said I lacked imagination, but he said it in a friendly way, smiling as if I were a schoolboy who had failed to develop.

"Will you come to my home? I will cook you a meal and give you my books."

Why not?

As we got up, Nadiryan put his hand on my arm to steady himself.

"I have tuberculosis of the bones. Nothing to worry about."

I said that I wasn't worried.

We walked slowly down the street; it wound up hill, turning toward the Eglise St-Trophime.

"You see," Nadiryan pointed to the portal, there are the damned, chained and driven to hell. "You see how stoical they are, all but one, he is crying out—in fear perhaps, or grief—Dante would approve. But these images are repulsive. The world they knew was full of despair, but we are sinners, and there is nothing to be done about it. I am the one crying out, that one, bearded and shaking my fist at God."

"Is evil God's fault?"

"Of course. You know Dante, so you know Aquinas?"

"Yes, Augustine, Anselm, Aquinas, Scotus, Bonaventure, Francis. Catholic school."

We were standing under the portal. I helped Nadiryan to sit down on the stone steps below the wide door, with its austere saints carved in relief, its corbel heads and tapering pillars. Though I had come to Arles to pay my respects to Van Gogh, the discovery of the great Romanesque church, with it cloister and gardens, was like a balm easing the ache of memory, the images and dreams that had haunted me for the past three years. These churches were reminders of the immensity of human desire, of the search for order and happiness. I had no desire to worship in them, but their grave beauty seemed hopeful.

Nadiryan told me that Saint Thomas Aquinas had an argument for the goodness of things rooted in the idea of divine providence. God is pure intellect; the intellect of God is purely good; the world that God has made is there- fore rational, divinely infused, and good. Aquinas believed that will and intellect are one. That is a remarkable idea I think, since it supposes that what God wishes to be the case is the case, so that the world is the pure manifestation of divinity. Not far from Spinoza in thinking that the world embodies God and is therefore wholly good.

But, I said, Spinoza appeals to me more. He felt the oneness of things and fought against the idea of evil by making God and the world one substance. It was a lost fight, but he had great courage.

"Yes," Nadiryan said, "Spinoza was a great heretic, an outcast from every community. No thinker was ever more alone. Tell me what you think about this. He wrote that there is no affection of the body about which we could not have clear knowledge. In other words, we are able to know ourselves, just as Socrates commanded us to do."

Nadiryan had kind eyes. I couldn't hold his look and had no idea how to explain my ideas to him. I had never thought about his question so I said that I think that the world is evil, that men are wicked, and that if God exists he has made himself into a kind of puzzle, like a great king who presides over the land of the damned.

"You are wrong. The world is neither good nor evil. The evil is apparent to us because it appears to overpower what is good, it makes up the story that is called history, but if we were omniscient, seeing as God sees, then the good that ordinary people do each day would far outweigh evil. Men are capable of great wickedness, yes, but Augustine was wrong about inherent sin. Are men alone wicked? Are children at the breasts of their mothers capable of evil? No my friend, we become evil out of fear of one another. Yes there is sinfulness, but what does that mean? That God has erred in making us afraid of our brothers, but also afraid of life. And God has nothing to answer for; in any case, to whom shall he answer? To man, whose wickedness you admit? To Himself, who is all things, whose will is act, whose intellect is the reason why there is something rather than nothing? What would we do without some hope that human misery has meaning? That is why these images are repulsive and your Dante a fraud. Life is not a theatre, with good and evil characters struggling toward some resolution. All that matters is taking place right now, here between us, and everywhere we are not. Evil is being done right now, and acts of kindness, and gestures that are neither, but which are necessary to sustain us. Your poet, the Puritan Milton, is a reductionist. The world is too vast, too complicated, to be encompassed by a narrow vision of heaven and hell."

"And what about your life? Are you satisfied?" It seemed a bold question, but I couldn't help myself.

"One life signifies nothing. The life a of people matters, traditions. No one life can be more important than the collective lives of a people."

"No, not at all. Only the life of the person has value. Imagine the suffering of one of those men of stone there on the portal. See, that one, imagine that he is an adulterer, a man who once loved his wife and adored his children but for reasons that he does not understand he went with another woman—for pleasure, for a moment of pleasure. And yet this is a grave sin. He is being dragged to hellfire for eternity. For the sin of sex outside of marriage. Absurd. Not only because the punishment is so much in excess of the crime, but because we cannot know what desperation drove this figure of stone to betray his vow. I oppose morality that ignores this fact, that the mystery of the individual's life comes before anything else."

Nadiryan was silent, and we both sat and looked up at the great door, with its commentary on eternity.

———·∿·———

[2012]: Early in the war, the Armenians of northern Turkey knew that they would be murdered. The *mutessarif* of Moush announced to the world that the Turks would kill all Armenians at the first moment of the war: "We will exterminate the race." Ekran Bey, in an audience with the American and German Consuls to Ankara, declared the Turkish government's intentions in regard to the Armenian people—they would be exterminated. Max Scheubner-Richter, the German vice Consul in Erzurum was told by Erzincanli Sabit that "all the Armenians in Turkey will be killed; they have become a menace to the Turkish race; their extermination is the only remedy." There would be "no Armenians left alive in Turkey after the war." The German vice-Consul has left no notes of his conversations with the Turkish leadership. Perhaps he did not believe that a million men, women, and children could so simply be "exterminated." Or perhaps he did, and found the actions of the Turks instructive. There was much to learn in the Orient, according to Scheubner-Richter. The year was 1914.

I suppose Nadiryan is still alive, living and writing in Arles. I think of him sometimes. Here is one of his poems, translated for me by a grad student here at Penn: "This sullen land holds the bones of multitudes,/The earth no longer contains our dead/Our desert sea washes our ancestors clean—Turk and Greek—they rest as one/Our people too are broken into pieces, ground into sand, washed by the pitiless sun/In life we are forced to weep, but at the ends of the earth/Here in this antipode, we too may rest."

[Still 2012]: Thinking all these years later about Nadiryan's poem, and the word 'antipode' in particular. Here is something I wrote a month ago. Was I anticipating this moment, the mention of Alice, her dying? There is something eerie in the connections I am finding in these texts, something that suggests foresight and prophecy. Alice and I were *connected*, that much is clear. Could I feel her all this time, did I know she was dead before I read the obituary?

Here's the thought: Did Christ visit the antipodes? [Cambodia] This was a question posed by St. Augustine. The antipodes were uninhabited, so Christ was spared the trip, but then this wasn't everyone's view. Alexander Neckham, writing in the middle of the thirteenth century, thought that the antipodes were occupied by a people who lived their lives upside-down and backward—how else would they live? [I was thinking about immigrants. I remember reading a story in the *Journal* about the Wall, about turning away people from Central America]. Turn the world upside down, and language flies backward as well. When I first heard Vietnamese it seemed to me antipodean, a slurry of vowels and gutturals attached to no meaning, an angry voice as foreign to me as the unbearable air and sunlight like broken glass. The Vietnamese were slight and their faces were closed to me. Their heads not quite in their chests as Mandeville imagined, but faces whose blandness made me afraid. [The Other!] Dante, famously, froze Satan in a sea of ice—ice!—in the middle of the universe, that is, at the furthest point from God, and put a sinner into each of the Great Beast's three maws. The antipodes, frozen in ice or burning in fire, imagined as a world never to be seen, yet Marco Polo, with Ibn Battuta, history's greatest traveler, walked to the other side of the world. Polo called his book *Il Milione*. Nicolo, father of Marco, and Nicolo's uncle Maffio resided at first in the great city of Constantinople, but left just before the city was conquered by Michael Palaeologus—a Nicaean king who blinded all resident Venetians. The Polos reached Dadu, or Beijing, in 1266 where they met Kublai Khan. According to the *Travels*, Kublai Khan requested a hundred Christian missionaries to bring the truth of Christianity to his Kingdom. Marco, his father, and his great-uncle returned to China, to Mongolia, in 1274. Marco lived in China for seventeen years. The young Marco was trusted by the Khan, to such an extent that Polo became an emissary to the court. When he finally returned to Venice in 1299, no one believed his stories. He died at age seventy. His book, in the Latin versions, was annotated by Columbus and probably led the intrepid and vainglorious Genoan to undertake his western voyage. The VP rare book room had a charming image [I can see it clearly even now] taken from a collection of medieval marginalia—in red and blue *tempera*—of the Polos disembarking from an impossibly tiny single-masted caravel into an impossibly tiny castle. There is an odd white elephant in the caravel and a dromedary standing outside the fortress. Nothing is to scale, but the image makes its point—here they are arrived in the Mysterious

East. I looked at this image many times and imagined the hand of the monk who painstakingly drew it, and imagined the eyes and the minds of the monks who looked at it for evidences of God's wonderful workings. Perhaps the castle was Armenian, or belonged to the ancestors of the people who wandered from the Caucasuses to Erzurum, Tercan, Erzincan, Trabzon, and the other towns of the Turkish highlands. The Polos might have been standing at Batum, on the southern rim of the Black Sea, or Izmir, where Agamemnon disembarked with his armies to burn the stately towers of Ilium. Priam begging Achilles for the life of his son. In old books, anything is possible.

I first became interested in Marco Polo when I happened upon *Invisible Cities*, by Italo Calvino.

Polo led me to Colon's letters.

The letters led me to Bernal Diaz.

Diaz, eventually, to Álvar Núñez Cabeza de Vaca's fantastical account of his journey—Marco Polo turned upside down. More antipodes. The man with the head of a cow was stranded on the shore of Spanish Florida—I would imagine in the great bay that now divides Tampa and St. Petersburg—hunted by the Seminole, he trekked northward into the panhandle, then west, for twenty-five hundred miles, across the swamps of the deepest southland, across the Mississippi—but how?—and then, impossibly, through the deadly heat of south Texas, crossing the great plain that now bears the city of Houston, named, of course, for Sam, first governor of Tejas, opponent of slavery, a man of outsized ambitions, American to his bones. Cowhead walked across the flinty creosote desert of Nuevo Mexico, finally reaching the Rio Grande, then, of course, not a dry sandy arroyo but a river bursting with the melted snows of the Sierra Madre del Norte, the Sangre de Cristos, the deepest reaches of the great backbone of mountains that flow from the Bering sea to Patagonia. And, at last, after the Biblical seven years had elapsed, Cabeza de Vaca reached Mexico City—where no one believed his tales, just as no one believed Polo or the great explorer Ibn Battuta, who saw more of the earth than any other man, and who wrote about what he had seen in his own book of marvels. Antipodes! Who comes close to these great travel writers? Bruce Chatwin, whose account of his voyage to Patagonia shines with the intelligence of Battuta; Rebecca West, whose journeys in the Balkans astound me. Back and forth, across time and space, among the believers and the heathen, the world of words moves as a great fire in the minds of human beings. Whatever there is might be other than it is, might be upside down, or reversed, or spoken in a language that no one understands, one that has not yet been invented. My own antipodes, Nadiryan's, Vincent's, and Gauguin's in his demi-paradise, all of us carrying the world within our rotting bones. Tubercular.

[All of this is so strange, but there's a point to it: I was traveling back to my antipodes, back to Cambodia, hence to Alice].

Because of my great admiration for the Venetian merchant I read his book often, usually during my own rest-less travels. In Japan or Germany, in Vietnam or along the Ho Chi Minh trail in Cambodia, in the far reaches of northern New Jersey or the desolate rail yards of Philadelphia, I would dream of the unimaginable towns—their names a mantra of unworldliness: Guangzhou, Trebizond, the wastes beyond the Aral Sea, Madurai, Mylapore, and the mountainous plains of Aleppo, the Venice of the East. What thoughts must have stirred Polo as he made his journey? We know that he was afraid, and at times homesick, but, above all, his narrative conveys curiosity, a hunger for experience, a love of life in all its myriad forms that appears utterly at odds with the provincialism of the Middle Ages. Polo's hunger for experience became my own, his desperation for knowledge the pinnacle of human experience.

—————

[January 20, 1981]: I saw her again just now. I feel like I know her. She was on the steps this morning, now here in the stacks. The light is pushing against the window: the sun's a thief and robs the vast sea.

—————

Half-past-eleven. There's a conversation in progress around the corner near the study carrels occupied by the East Asia students. It sounds like an argument, though in a language I am not familiar with. Khmer, but not like Kuo Seng's. Stilted or educated, I can't tell. I peek around the corner. I knew before I looked that it was the woman from earlier. Dark hair, very pretty. The man is Cambodian. They are speaking earnestly. They both look up at me at once, feeling my eyes on them. Neither smiles. I point, stupidly, to the shelves near them; step forward, pretend to scan the call numbers, then pluck a book, in Korean, from the shelf. I mumble "sorry" and walk away.

I walk down to the stairwell and light a cigarette. The woman intrigues me. She is pretty, but it's not that. She is someone I am drawn toward, like the pole star on a dark night.

—◊—

Herodotus reports that when a corpse was brought to the embalmers they would make a wooden model of the body and paint it in a life-like way. There were three levels of detail, of life-likeness, in these models, graded by quality. After the models were completed, the kinsmen of the dead person were asked to choose which model suited their needs. Once they had chosen, the embalmers set to work fashioning the body to resemble the model that had been selected. The brain of the dead person was removed through the nostrils with a metal hook, and the emptied body cavity washed clean with palm wine and filled with aromatic spices. The stuffed corpse was then aged for seventy days—"never longer"—wrapped in linen, and returned to the family.

And: "Time in the wilderness" and "what is the meaning of this terrible freedom?" Emerson? From a review of *Confessions*? Surveying the landscape of American history one finds a surprising thread of anomie, melancholy— black bile clogging the life-sustaining veins. A life must be sketched in three dimensions to have substance: the physical (first dimension) afforded by the great landscape of the New World proved incapable of filling the inner void (dimension two) of those who were willing to look at it; the third dimension of a life is memory, the tallying up of what one has made of afforded chances. Think of all the ways

one can categorize a person's life—well, there are many—
but the only one that matters is the memory created by that
life—memory is a hole in time, a void that is left when the
pliers draw out the soul.

One imagines that the cheapest model was carved by
apprentices and painted by an understudy. That there was
a first time for doing a body on one's own and that mistakes
are sometimes made. The stuffing is cajuput, frankincense,
and myrrh. Did the Magi come to praise or to embalm Him?

I am writing nonsense. I can't focus. Almost noon.

———

The inauguration of the President of the United States.
There is a photograph of Lincoln taking the oath of office
on the Capitol steps. As I recall, he towers above everyone
else, though even he is a fleck of black and gray in the
photo. There is a scaffolding attached to the dome, and
the crowd, though large, can't be distinguished—they are
just bodies arrayed before the massive marble steps. I have
stood on those steps half-a-dozen times, always imagining Lincoln. The view down the Mall is majestic, though
his own Memorial, the best part of the view, was in 1861
just a stand of trees, with the Potomac hidden by the crest
of a small hill. I imagine the scene at this moment as a
new President takes the oath of office, an oath that he will
certainly bend or break within a few months, and there are
a million people standing on the Mall, jubilant masses of
my fellow citizens, and the man has promised "the dawn of
a new era." We are hungry for hope.

———

Khmer. The Red Khmers. I remember when I first

heard the language. Somewhere west of Tay Nanh, deep in the jungle. The Lurps had taken three prisoners, NVA they assumed, but our interpreter told us they were Cambodian, Khmer Rouge. Nobody could understand what they were saying. The ARVN platoon leader attached to our unit just shrugged and said we should shoot them.

[**February 2012**]: We don't re-collect the past, we reimagine it.

[**February 2012**]: The first dead body I saw was lying half-covered on the tarmac at Cam Ran Bay airfield, April 13, 1968. The sun was baking hot and the air carried smells that set our stomachs on edge. The airport was alive with activity, men scurrying into and out of the bellies of C-130s, equipment being off-loaded by enormous fork-lifts, the roar of Hueys and a couple of Skycranes hauling gear upcountry, tired grunts filing onto planes to return to the States, and cherries like me just arriving for thirteen months of duty. Thirteen that stretched into three tours, thirty-six months. I was in-country right at the end of Tet. There were plenty of bodies around, plenty of war stories.

[**January 20, 1981**]: Freud has a beautiful, short essay "On Transience." He wrote it for a volume intended as an appreciation of the life and works of Goethe. The book was published during World War I and was intended to demonstrate to the world that Germans were not barbar-ians. "I could not see my way to dispute the transience of all things, nor could I insist upon an exception in favor of what is beautiful and perfect. But I did dispute the pessimistic poet's view that the transience of what is beautiful involves any loss in its worth." The poet was Rilke. The loss of beauty is to be expected, and not mourned—to have possessed beauty for even a moment is a miracle. Yet Freud is being obtuse here: mourning is not "a great riddle" but the cost of intelligence. "When once the mourning is over…" The pun is perfect, in English or in German. When the morning ends, so does love.

We strive to further the occurrence of whatever we imagine will lead to joy, and to avert or destroy what we imagine is contrary to it, or will lead to sadness. Spinoza.

A poet whom I admire, a long-lived Polish writer of versatility and profound experience, once wrote that one life is not enough to experience fully the sadness of this world. The same wind blows across us all. My mother, my grandfather who could no longer endure life. The friends I buried and the lives I took. Sweet-souled Vincent and an Armenian poet who kissed my cheek, the distant dead crowded in stone on the portals of great churches, the authors of these books and, sadly, I fear, the books themselves. These books, the names of their authors, the hopeful words they contain: passages through which I may enter the past or project myself into the future. *A poem,* another Polish poet wrote, ***could contain the whole world.*** Which means that some combination of words might exist that describes everything that is past or present or to come. Perhaps this poem is here, somewhere in the **PR-PZ** range of the Van Pelt Library, or across the way in the BFs, lying unread on the bottom of a darkened range that hasn't been visited for fifty years. Perhaps I will find it.

It's getting late. There are a few things that need to be done. Dazed, I hustle downstairs to the poetry section—there isn't a poetry section. The poets find themselves shelved with colleagues who write prose and travel books and sociology: language seems to be the organizing principle. Since there isn't one single place where I can find my favorite poets I've created my own shelf of poetry, down in the deepest darkest corner of the bottom floor, the back edge of the undusted shelves that contain massive uniformly-bound books of agricultural and educational and demographic surveys—sad bricks of books that no one has ever looked at, so old that the little LC call number stickers on their edges have been filled out with a fountain pen, back when Harding was president. These books smell like Canadian forests, full of dried pulp and ink made from lamb's blood. They stick together on the shelves—like those who have sinned grievously—so that when you pull one down at random (*Lancaster Country Farm Production: Dairy Section, 1919*) it clings to its shelf mates, cracking like the sharp ice that girds the oaks on the quad, coming away half sticky with that deep burgundy that library binders seem to prefer. Here, I open to page 564, Paradise (Unincorporated) surveys, cows outnumbering Amish dairymen five to one; tons of manure produced, tons of corn consumed, gallons (in thousands) shipped: a world of facts whose contours are shaped by black earth and dawn milking in freezing barns, lanky men with zipper-less overalls and wide-brimmed straw hats, Lincoln beards, coats too light for the black cold, unschooled children in tiny mucking boots trailing behind (the kitchens still warm with wood fires and fresh bread, pitchers of milk and plates thick with yellow butter). "The pine-trees crusted with snow." The dusty smell of these unloved volumes makes me dizzy, gleeful, to think of the work and the archival concern to preserve events that had so little significance to anyone outside of the tiny towns that tourists visit only to gawk at the Anabaptists and to buy their cheap but serviceable furniture. Here it is. What was on my mind all morning. . . .

At the earliest ending of the winter,
In March, a scrawny cry from outside
Seemed like a sound in his mind.

....

Surrounded by its choral rings,
Still far away. It was like
A new knowledge of reality.

There is never enough time. I gather up my notebooks and stuff them into my bag. Happiness comes to us in unexpected ways. The stairs lead only up, up into the wash of voices on the floors above. My leg aches, but gently. I pay attention to the faces of those I pass, to the quiet activity of the reading room.

As I push through the doors into the thin light of late morning I thought the black boughs of this white oak would crack in the cold wind. It is starting to snow. The quad is empty. I button my pea coat and head east.

⁓⁓⁓

[2012]: What a mess. Even adding dates where I was sure of them doesn't unscramble these random jottings. But reading them over has reawakened memories that I believed were lost forever. Obviously I didn't write all of the above—fifty notebook pages—in one morning or even in a single day. I made some notes and then I added to them, filled out the account of the day, of what I was doing and thinking about. Some of what I wrote about my grandfather is fabricated, part of a fictional memoir. But there it is, the first part of the "Alice notebook." The trips to Japan were real, but I can't remember anything about them—the stories might be true. My frame of mind is what interests me as I go back through this material, and it seems important to recreate some context so that I can make sense of what I am feeling now—that I may have had one chance in my life to be happy and that I refused to take it. Why? The answer to that question is here.

What follows is Alice's story, in her words, and mine.

January 20, 1981

Alice finished her meal and washed the dishes. Living alone had deepened her habits of neatness and order. Her apartment was small but well-maintained, the walls hung with Navaho rugs that she had collected during a year in Santa Fe. There were *retratos* above her books—primitive carvings of the Virgin and of St. Francis that she had purchased from a craftsman who worked near the *santurario* in Chimayo. Each time she looked at the rough wood of the icons she remembered the day she had seen them in the workshop of Jorge Sanchez. The *Sangre de Cristos* were covered in snow and the sky was pure blue. She walked into the shop and watched as Sanchez whittled the cowled head of Francis. After a while the artist smiled at her and asked if she would like to see other work. There was a small room full of carvings, each as different as the pilgrims who passed through the doors of the church next door—"I carve the God who lives in all his children." Alice said nothing, but she purchased two pieces. They were peaceful in the dim January light.

Alice's mother had died a few weeks before Christmas. She wasn't shocked. Her mother's death was expected, overdue, and Alice, who was on intimate terms with the dead, was saddened but not surprised. Her telephone rang in the middle of the night. Her father was incoherent. Alice drove home to New Jersey to make the funeral arrangements. Dying had taken Alice's mother half a year—her father was nearly dead himself. There were no brothers and sisters, no aunts and uncles—the Nye's had lived in isolation, reinforced by blue-collar paranoia. Once an anomalous way of living, now, increasingly, the norm. Lonely people cut off from the world and afraid of things that once gave us comfort. The government above all else. The government that would come for Bob's guns, or build a homeless shelter next door, or discover a rich seam of coal running through the middle of their land, so there were no next-door neighbors, and their land was surrounded by a tall fence and protected by a pack of dogs. Overkill, since the Nye's lived in the middle of nowhere, in the Pine Barrens, an enormous wilderness in the southern counties of the most congested and overpopulated state, ten miles outside of Batso on the Mullica River.

The house, ramshackle at its best, was falling into ruin. Alice's mother's room smelled stale—of camphor and decay. As she looked at her mother's empty bed, Alice imagined her own body lying there—she saw herself in place of her mother and thought how mothers might wish to die for their children but that daughters seldom thought to return the favor. Her father was sitting in the living room in front of a fire that Alice had made, drinking bourbon out of a jelly jar. The air that pushed through the flimsy walls felt like glass, the walls were brittle and creaked in the wind.

After she had called the funeral home and arranged for her mother to be cremated, Alice went into her old room and shut the door. She lay on her old bed and fell into a deep sleep. In her dreams Alice was running through a jungle of living plants. Each time she pulled at one of the vines that clung to her legs, the soft green tissue would break and a thick viscous liquid would pour out and cover her. She brushed at the blood of the plants that stained her skin. In the moments before she awoke (it seemed), Alice came to a lake that was surrounded by ashes—and she knew that the ashes stood for her mother's remains and wondered how she could be thinking about those ashes while still asleep—how her mind could watch its own images even while unconscious—but she also knew, somehow, that in dreams such splits are possible—and when she had figured this out, she jumped into the still water of the lake and woke up.

⌁

After lunch, Alice put on her coat and bicycled through blackened snow to her campus office. It was chilly in her cubicle, but she felt calm whenever she sat at her desk. Some days she'd go to the library and work, do her translations or read history. Some days she would leave her bicycle at the University and take long walks downtown. On Saturdays she might go to a movie or a concert. She never planned her days, but lived them automatically, thoughtlessly.

Alice's desk was piled high with books and off-prints of

articles, with photocopied drafts of her thesis, a bulky old Remington typewriter and pads of legal paper full of scribbles in English, French, and Khmer.

There was no hope that she would finish her dissertation or her degree, but she persisted in what she thought of, and described to others, as her "work." No professor would sponsor her project, nor would the philosophy department recognize its value. She was "kept on," as the chairman put it, because she was the only graduate student who would cheerfully teach required introductory courses to disinterested undergraduates. The department's professors were preoccupied with their own research in what the chairman called "issues of concern for this community of scholars." This judgment, and her marginal status, did not bother Alice. All she had wanted was time to think, a stipend, and anonymity. When Alice had rejoined the world of ordinary endeavors—when she had left behind the land of the dead—what she wished for was a sanctuary. In her mind, universities stood for purity of motive and clarity of intention. She knew this wasn't true, but it was easier to believe it than to find another place in which to carry on her life.

Alice's "topic" was forgetting.

———

During the week that she spent at home in the Pine Barrens with the memory of her mother, Alice caught up on her sleep and reading. She finished *Memoirs of an Anti-Semite* and read *First Love*, Turgenev's early novel. She also read fiction by Pech Sanwawann and Say Khun in Khmer, and made some translations. She read poems by

Vallejo and Parrera in Spanish, though her knowledge of that language was imperfect. She wrote letters to her dead mother, and she looked after her father.

The weight of the rooms in her childhood home, their emptiness, kept Alice from any real work—her memory project sat on the desk she had used as a child. There seemed little point in doing anything productive, in trying to stoke the dying embers of her ambition—at the moment, the death of her mother had made everything seem pointless.

Her second evening at home, after her father was in bed, Alice locked the door to her room and took off her clothes. She laid pictures of her mother—a wedding portrait, old family shots taken around the house and at the shore, yellowed Kodak snapshots of her mother holding Alice or smiling at her husband—and spread them out on the bed. Then Alice lay down on top of the pictures. She closed her eyes and concentrated on the feeling of the images on her body. The sensation was visceral. Alice felt like she was hallucinating the past as flowing scenes, silent and jerky, awkward as home movies, flowed across her closed eyes. She rubbed the photos across her stomach and breasts and, for the first time since her mother had died, she wept.

<hr>

Alice had won a scholarship to Georgetown University. It was her intention to study politics and international relations. She wasn't particularly interested in these subjects, but then she wasn't interested in any one thing, and felt as if the compartmentalizing of knowledge was a distraction from the pleasure of learning things for their own sake. Her upbringing and irregular education, her lack of discipline, had led her to believe that reading in the public library would provide a sufficient introduction to the world, and that college wasn't a place one went to learn but a place one went to socialize—to do the kind of things that she had avoided doing in high school. Nothing from her past had prepared her to think in terms of a career, and she had no intention of wasting her time acquiring job skills. Her mother had homeschooled Alice until she was fourteen. Her erratic and disorganized education hadn't covered a standard curriculum, but it had stoked Alice's curiosity. Her mother had put into Alice's hands books from the family's odd-ball, sixties-hippie collection—classic English novels and the works of Richard Brautigan, John McPhee and Annie Dillard; books about the natural world; standard texts of philosophy deeply annotated by her mother, who had majored in the subject at Glassboro State; histories of the Civil War beloved by her father, and lots of practical Whole-Earth-Catalogue-style materials — how to build a yurt, how to dress a deer, how to load your own ammunition. She and her mother had been inseparable. The family's isolation in the Pine Barrens enforced closeness between mother and daughter. Alice's mother had taught her daughter cooking and sewing and gardening. Alice knew how to can vegetables and could play the recorder; her father taught her how to fly fish and to identify edible plants and the major constellations. She could run wild, and she did—being independent was the point of her family's existence, the reason they were comfortable living without any of the amenities of modern life. For her parents the only amenity worth having was independence.

When Alice turned fourteen, her mother and father decided, reluctantly, to send her to high school in Lumberton. They understood that Alice was bright and would learn more in a formal setting—if not more, then at least some of the things that they were not equipped to teach her. And they worried that their daughter had no friends. It was one thing for them to live a solitary existence, but it seemed cruel to cut their child off from the world. Alice would have preferred to remain at home, and she was indifferent to the prospect of having friends her own age. But high school was good for her, and she was bright. The discipline of regular schooling, even in a run-of-the-mill public high school, deepened her habits of study and reflection. Alice didn't make many friends, and she didn't fit in with any of the cliques at Lumberton High, but she did learn a great deal—French and Spanish, how to write and debate, and, in particular, she learned to love the 'panorama'—as it was called—of history thanks to a dedicated older teacher who had been waiting for a student like Alice all her life. Alice graduated with highest honors and, with the encouragement of her history teacher, applied to three colleges—two state schools and Georgetown. Her teacher, Ms. Hale, had gone there, and she told Alice that not only was it a fine university but it was in a city that offered a rich range of possibilities for someone as curious and full of potential as Alice.

To Alice's surprise and delight, she was accepted at all

three schools and received generous financial aid from Georgetown. Her father was unenthusiastic about his daughter's living in the capital city of the corrupt republic, but he was overridden by his wife.

⸺∾∾⸺

During her sophomore year at Georgetown, Alice applied for and was awarded a grant by the Fulbright Foundation to travel to Asia. Most students visited Japan. Alice chose to spend a year in Cambodia. Her adviser at Georgetown attempted to dissuade her and pointed out the risks of visiting a country that bordered Vietnam and which was itself in the midst of civil turmoil. Alice was determined. She knew something about Buddhism, and she had read the history of Angkor Wat, but, above all, she wanted to experience a world that was as different from New Jersey as possible. Americans knew little about Cambodia and few people outside of the State Department spoke Khmer. Alice was persistent. She secured a recommendation from chair of the Department of International Studies that pointed out the enrichment opportunities afforded the college by virtue of having established a relationship with the Royal College of Cambodia.

Alice located a young woman named Khanlehanna Seng at American University and began to study the Khmer language and the history of Cambodia. At the end of August, 1967, she flew via Tokyo to Phnom Penh where she was enrolled as a special student at the Royal College. Her classes were in French, English, and Khmer. Alice lived in a dormitory, and she made friends among her Cambodian and French classmates. The work was difficult,

102

the language impossible, but she read widely, traveled a little and cultivated a deep affection for the beauty of the country, for its Buddhist traditions, and for the unworldly temple architecture.

Upon her return to Georgetown in the spring of 1968 Alice changed her major to Asian Studies, with a focus on the Khmer language and history of Southeast Asia. Because no one at Georgetown taught Khmer, Alice enrolled in a course taught at the State Department by an émigré whose family had moved from Cambodia to France during World War II, and then to Washington in the 1950s. Her interest in Asia deepened, and she planned to apply to the State Department for a job working in East Asia. Other things, unplanned, unimagined, intervened, but, in the end, she did travel to Phnom Penh, arriving in 1971. She remained until the end.

———~~~———

Not long before Christmas, with the sky slate gray and hanging just above the white pines, Alice went for a walk in the woods. The Pine Barrens are a strange place, dream-like in their emptiness. Fire created the pine tracts that dominate the Barrens. The ground is bare in winter; here and there are patches of snow hidden from the sun. In the spring the sandy ground is covered with white gentians and the smell of pitch fills the air.

This was where Alice had grown up. Her mother had taken her to gather blueberries in the summer, and they had collected pine cones to make feeders for the siskins and white-crowned sparrows that overwintered in their yard. Alice's parents had grown up in Mullica, gone to

103

school in Hammonton, married, and built a house in the woods with their own hands when they were barely in their twenties. They lived off the grid, without a phone or television. Alice had been born at home. Living off of the land, as Alice's father was fond of saying, was what made a person whole. He'd never read Jefferson, but Bob Nye was an instinctive Jeffersonian. In his view, no one in a city knew what hardship meant, or tranquility. The only virtue a person has comes through contact with the earth. It was a romantic view, but in that era, the Age of Aquarius, a reasonable one. When Alice was young she believed in the woods in the way other children believe in God or characters in movies.

Walking through the bitter cold, Alice spoke to her mother—

You've left at a bad time. You've left me alone when I needed advice. I hope you didn't suffer at the end. Dad told me that you were brave, that you didn't complain— you never complained. I'm sorry I wasn't here, but you understand. I couldn't see you those last months. I wouldn't have recognized you. I wasn't brave enough. Remember that you told me that this world isn't a perfect place, but that we have a duty to live. You can tell me now—are we only our bodies? I never believed in ghosts, but I'd like to know that you are one. Can you see where I am, half-way to Cog's House, the walk we took every Saturday in the winter, the long winding path to the frozen creek, where we would gawk at the spirals of ice on the rocks, and I would break a piece off and give it to you as if it were a diamond and you would dutifully carry it home—three miles of carrying ice in your mittened hands—a sliver of ice; you held it until it broke or it melted. Thinking about the ice drives me mad. It makes me angry that you are dead. *I hope you aren't afraid.*

Alice felt foolish speaking out loud to her mother. She knew death was nothingness. Death didn't frighten Alice, nor had it frightened her mother, and yet it was unbearable to think that she would never again in all the eternity of worlds drink a cup of coffee with the one person she had loved unconditionally.

⁓⁓⁓

On this day, the 20th of January, a day that was rich in associations for Alice, her mother's birthday, Alice sat in her austere office compiling her record of the destruction of Cambodia.

"I awoke each morning before dawn and rode my bicycle to the factory. Later, after my father had passed away, I took a second job selling noop bangchop—*food for the poor. At the time of the revolution, in April, 1975, I was working as a caretaker in the Buddhist temple of Wat Kandal, in Battambang province, my home. I was arrested by the Khmer Rouge and charged with being a spy for Lon Nol.*

The first interrogations took place a week after my arrest. I was taken to a room in the temple and beaten by several cadres. They asked me nothing. After they beat me I was tied to a board, standing upright. One soldier–he was just a peasant boy, like me–wound wire around my stomach and shocked me by turning a crank. I could smell my flesh burning. After a while, I passed out.

Later I was taken to the prison at Tuol Sleng. There were thousands of men and women there. The guards carried people screaming into the torture rooms, using water to make them gag—to nearly drown them. We were given food twice a day, a few teaspoons of rice porridge. We huddled in tiny rooms—the prison was a school building—waiting for our turn. Some were stoical and silent, some wept, and some of us went mad. I thought that I was in hell, that I had fallen into a deep sleep and gone on a voyage to the netherworld, a world of unrelieved terror."

Near the end of her manuscript, a bulky typescript that Alice had worked on for a decade, she inserted a letter written by Prince Sirik Matak to the American Ambassador, John Gunther Dean, a letter written as Cambodia fell to the Khmer Rouge. In some ways this short note captured the despair that had settled on the doomed nation in those last months, a time that Alice could not forget:

Dear Excellency and friend,

I thank you very sincerely for your letter and for your offer to transport me towards freedom. I cannot, alas, leave in such a cowardly fashion.

As for you and in particular for your great country, I never believed for a moment that you would have this sentiment of abandoning a people which has chosen liberty. You have refused us your protection and we can do nothing about it. You leave us and it is my wish that you and your country will find happiness under the sky.

The Prince was executed early in May, 1975, on orders from Pol Pot.

"It is my wish that you and your country will find happiness under the sky." These words haunted Alice. They were graceful and bespoke a vast compassion, and they were also ironic and unbearable. During the years that Alice worked for the State Department in Cambodia she had gradually come to understand the Buddhist view of the vast scope of time, a view that renders all human actions insignificant. She hadn't become a fatalist, but she had unclenched her heart—Alice knew that desire is folly and that our wishes are as insubstantial as the wind now stirring the black oaks outside her office window. Her mother had come to this understanding as well, not through Buddhist thought, but through what Alice called 'cancer mind.' Her mother hadn't 'gotten cancer,' she had *become* cancer, or it had become her. From the moment her lymphoma was diagnosed there was nothing in her mother's life that wasn't transformed by the disease—her identity, her being, all became something other than what they had been. When Alice visited her, she looked for the person who had raised her—and she was there, but not there, as if her flesh had been compressed and flattened. Alice's stoicism vanished in those first moments when she kissed her mother's parchment lips and held a hand colder than flesh should ever be. Alice had seen death before, more than most people, but nothing prepared her for the vanishing of the woman she had known.

The beauty of the Prince's remark was the final phrase "under the sky." This made sense to Alice. If the realm of possible happiness was as wide as the sky, then surely it could be found. Happiness is in this world. Happiness not in Kampuchea or the worn-out split level on the Mullica River, but somewhere.

—◦◦◦—

"Hey Alice, what's going on?"

"I'm writing. Translating actually."

"Yeah, I can see that. I was more asking what you're writing."

"I'm translating the testimonies of some survivors of the prison at Tuol Sleng; more precisely, if you like, I'm collecting testimonies that could be used to prosecute a criminal named Kaing Guek Eav. He is guilty of genocide. He ran the torture house and murdered at least ten thousand people. Caused to be murdered."

"Sounds depressing."

"That's true."

"Not that other things aren't."

Alice hadn't looked up from her work. "Many things are, yes. But this writing has an urgency that goes beyond what I feel about it. If that makes sense."

"You know Cambodian?"

"Khmer, yes, yes I do."

"May I ask how? I mean, it's not like French or German."

"No it isn't. I learned a little in college. Then I lived in Cambodia for a while."

"So can I ask you why you're doing this translating if you're in fact a graduate student in philosophy? That is, if you are, as I believe, what you are." If it were possible, Lee's words felt as if they emerged shrouded in a smirk.

Alice had no use for Lee or for others like him. He had been hanging around in graduate school for a decade, allegedly writing a dissertation on Wittgenstein, earning a miserable stipend, teaching introductory classes, enjoying free coffee and subsidized lunches. He was dull in the way that schooled but uneducated people are dull.

"You may ask, yes."

Lee thought Alice was attractive, but aloof. He would have described her, as he had on several occasions to his fellow grad students, as 'bitchy but probably worth it,' though he had no knowledge that could have justified his view. Philosophers think no more clearly about ordinary life than anyone else; perhaps less clearly. In Lee's eyes, Alice had *been around*, though no one knew where, and she had the look of self-possession that was unnerving—most of her colleagues kept their distance. The Chair called her Greta Garbo, but not to her face. Lee had no interest in her work, but he enjoyed the contact. He lived, as most people do, vicariously.

"With your permission then, Ms. Nye, I ask."

Alice finally turned around and faced Lee. He was a pale man with thick hair—he looked like Schopenhauer.

Alice wondered if she should bother answering. She offered a short version of what she was doing, more for her own sake then his. "Have you noticed how every philosopher starts over again? The same questions, the same pseudo-problems? And how they appear to forget what words mean when they argue with their predecessor—that is, the ones who bother with their predecessors? And how they appear never to have read a word of history? To ignore history—there's a philosopher's trick. The problem I'm working on is the philosophy of forgetting. Why do we do it? I believe we forget consciously—does that sound odd?—but we do. We make a pact with the past to let it go, to forgive by forgetting. Cambodia, and especially the Khmer Rouge, the genocide that began in 1975—that is my case study. Do you want to know something remarkable? Here's a philosophical truth for you to ponder Lee, *the Cambodian people themselves forgot the past, even before it happened.*"

"What are you talking about?"

"Think about it. People have to be prepared to remember, they have to live outside of myth, in the real world of cruelty, in order to comprehend what is happening to them. Prince Sihanouk—you know who he was don't you?—created a fantasy world in his extraordinary country, a world where time had no meaning, and therefore where history could not exist. You'll have to take my word for it. The consequences of such disregard were catastrophic."

"A muddled line of argument Alice. Richter would say you were spinning your ontological wheels. Time always exists; so does causality. It's just wrong to say a whole country has forgotten."

"Forgive me for saying so, but Richter is hardly an authority on reality. No matter. What took place in

Cambodia from 1975 to 1979 is unforgettable, yet forgotten. And I ask—why? Or, how? In the work I have been doing, I provide the testimonies and biographies of some of the victims. Think about it Lee, forget logic for a minute," and Alice gave Lee a glimpse into her passion, "think about the victims of history. The ordinary people swept up in the historical events we celebrate—The Great War, or decolonization—there's one for you Lee, you can read a book on decolonization and not find a word about the victims, I mean, you get the numbers, millions of them, ordinary people like us, people with hopes and dreams who get ground into dust by history, but that's all you get, numbers. I'm looking at a couple of hundred people in my work, men and women, children, whose stories I have pieced together. They stand for perhaps two million others—*two million human beings*, as many as live in this city. The people of doomed Cambodia, a country that didn't understand that it was doomed, that forgot its own future. Think of it."

"I have to admit that I haven't thought about it, I mean, about Cambodia. I don't know anything about it."

"There you go." Alice was sick of talking. She had work to do.

"But Alice is this relevant? I mean, it's interesting and all, compelling even, but what you're doing doesn't sound like philosophy, it's more like, I don't know, politics."

"Who cares? I mean, honestly Lee, who gives a damn what I do?"

⁓

Alice had married too young, while a junior at Georgetown, married a professor, a man twenty years older

111

than she, someone she thought she admired. She confused admiration for love. Or perhaps she did love him—who can say?

In any case she was innocent when she arrived in Washington from the New Jersey woods. Bright and driven, prone to brief, intense infatuations, both intellectual and emotional. She wasn't a virgin when she got to college, but she knew nothing about her heart. Sex was like reading: it opened up realms of feeling that were too powerful to resist. Alice thought she might be a poet or a painter, someone who condensed the complexities of experience into memorable forms, and this ambition seemed to justify her experiments with other bodies and other minds. She admired the artists on display in the National Gallery—the first art she had ever seen—and, in particular, was moved by the intense experiments of the abstract expressionists, their ideas about how feeling can be condensed into color—Rothko and De Kooning and Pollack in particular—and these artists made Alice aware of how narrow her own perception of meaning was, how limited her range of feeling. A classmate suggested she read Kandinsky's treatise on the spiritual component of art, and, having done so, she stepped over the line that had been drawn through her life since she was a child. Every person lives in nature but not every person lives for it—Alice had been brought up to think of the natural world and her place in it as formative, and to see art and music and literature as a diversion. After the National Gallery and Kandinsky and a couple of freshman courses, Alice crossed a line—this was how it seemed to her—into an embrace of the artificial, the yearning for "truth."

Her first real teacher, a young Freudian—a scholar attracted to the philosophical rather than to the therapeutic possibilities of psychoanalysis—a thinker whose lectures were filled with auditors, had been born in New York and received his Ph.D. from Harvard. He was, in every way, the opposite of Alice—urbane, cultured, upper-middle class, and cynical. Turley, as he preferred to be called, allowed the students from his introductory classes to come to his house for coffee, jug wine and discussions, an invitation Alice declined at first out of shyness, but then, shielded by her classmates, she decided to breach the walls of Turley's home, a tidy box of a place filled with books and records, with paintings and posters. Turley kept his house open at all times, to students of all philosophical and political inclinations. People dropped in, and if Turley had other things to do, he simply went about his business. He wasn't Socrates—he didn't have any personal investment in the students who sat on his Salvation Army couches, nor did he invite anyone to his home out of loneliness—they just came, and he neither welcomed nor discouraged their presence. He was one of those teachers who only care for the subject, not for the rolling parade of half-interested young people with whom he felt little connection.

Graduate students presided over the kitchen and liquor cabinet. They cooked the meals, cleaned up the dishes, and put away the records. They refereed arguments that sometimes threatened to become physical. Turley had an extensive collection of bebop LPs and *noir* mysteries, of baroque chamber music, long novels and short stories. And of course philosophy books—hundreds of them, more books than Alice had ever seen outside of a library—they lined every wall and were full of bits of paper, dog-eared and well read. The talk at Turley's was nearly always of philosophy, in particular, arguments about the work of Turley's own preferred thinkers—Freud and Jung, William James and John Dewey, the beloved John Stuart Mill, and also Hilary Putnam, Donald Davidson, and Richard Rorty—incisive, combative, iconoclastic one and all—and the Turley loyalists repeated their teacher's positions, quoting from his articles, defending his view that Freud was a moral thinker and that John Stuart Mill was a more important philosopher than the German neo-Hegelians whose metaphysics and view of history Turley found "fascistic," a preferred term of abuse in the days when public life was cast in terms of politics. It might have been the best time ever to be alive, to be a thinker, to be engaged. Or it might have been the worst.

Alice sat through a first long evening of talk that exceeded her understanding; Turley was there, quietly presiding, enjoying the life that flowed through his small living room and overflowed into the kitchen and backyard. Everyone drank beer or cheap wine, and even though Turley disliked drugs, he tolerated a dedicated group of potheads for the disjointed nonsense they brought to the discussions. Alice was stimulated, turned on by the camaraderie of the group. No preppies or jocks, just boys dressed in work clothes and heavy boots and girls in short skirts and oversized tee shirts. Everyone seemed mad for books in a way that Alice had not encountered before, and having had no real models of behavior to follow, she now became, slowly and without realizing it, a sort of thinker—a reader, a writer of some substance, someone who spent her days in a haze of ideas. She gave up casual encounters—both friends and lovers—and took care to guard her heart. Gradually she joined the cult of Dr. Turley—Philip—an uncritical follower of a modest man who enjoyed company and asked little of anyone; a man who was nobody's fool and nobody's confidant. More than anything, Turley was a provocation. As he put it, he provided the harmonic line, *basso continuo*, and let the others make the melody.

⁓

The next pages were typed on the back of flyers for a concert by a popular Philly band called 'Questionable Intent.' They were an early-80s Punk-Metal group that played at International House most Fridays, probably as a warning to foreign students to avoid American music. I caught their act once and didn't last twenty minutes. Aside from bleeding ears, I walked out with a backpack full of flyers–I always needed paper in those days. At some point, maybe in late '81 or '82, I imagined that I could write a novel about Alice's experiences in Cambodia. In those days the CIA was in the news a lot because of Nicaragua. Agents were training anti-communists in Honduras to destabilize the leftist government in Managua. It was a story that goes back to Iran and Guatemala and Cuba and the Congo–a long story. In this case the strategy worked better than usual, and by 1990 the Sandinistas were done for. Alice told me in a single crisp sentence that she "had some problems with the State Department when she returned to the

States," especially when she applied to the Thai government for a visa, apparently so that she could interview Cambodian refugees. The U.S. government closed the books on Southeast Asia in 1975, and anyone who wanted to go back there, especially anyone with Alice's history and clearance, was bound to be suspect. Anyway, that's what she told me. I did know a guy from the 82ⁿᵈ Airborne who claimed to have snuck back into Vietnam via Laos to rescue some Mnong who'd been attached to his unit. That's what he said. Then again you hear a lot of things that aren't true—it goes with the territory. War makes liars of honest men; and liars thrive in wartime. Here's my own contribution to the unraveling fabric of the past. My version of an important part of Alice's story, based on an imperfect recollection of things she told me.

"During the four days that Dan Karr and I (Don Welker) debriefed Alice Nye (who had, by that time, been legally divorced and readopted her maiden name), Ms. Nye was unwilling to share details of her life prior to her assignment at the Embassy in Phnom Penh. Ms. Nye was among the last to be extracted from the capital in April, 1975, and our employers considered her observations of the last months of Long Boret's regime to be of particular value. Ms. Nye was not an employee of the Agency; however, due to her facility in the Khmer language, she had been enlisted on several occasions to offer on-the-scene analyses of the deteriorating situation. Our relationship with her began in the spring of 1975. During several informal meetings that occurred late in May, meetings at which only Ms. Nye, Agent Karr, and I were present, Ms. Nye agreed to submit a written narrative of the circumstances of her life up to

116

the point of her deployment. In return she requested my cooperation in assisting her in obtaining a State Department visa that would allow her to return, with official standing, to Thailand, to the refugee camps then being constructed under the auspices of the UN. I was not empowered to make such an agreement, but promised Ms. Nye that the Agency would do all that it could—in recognition of her meritorious service during the period 1972-1975—to make the appropriate arrangements. Two weeks after these final meetings between Ms. Nye, Agent Karr, and me, I received the documents partially reprinted here. As should be obvious to the reader, Ms. Nye, for reasons known only to her, has chosen to submit in place of the requested factual account of her actions and contacts during the period from 1967 to 1971 a narrative focused primarily on her earlier life and on her marriage to Professor Philip Turley, at that time employed by Georgetown University (Attachment F). While the narrative submitted by Ms. Nye has little value as an evidentiary document—particularly in light of Ms. Nye's threat, made personally to me (see attachment C), a threat wholly unprovoked by either Agent Karr or myself, to release classified information in her possession [?] to Mr. Daniel Lucero of the *New York Times*—I nonetheless have attached it to Agent Karr's and my own notes on our official meetings of April and my notes, made after the fact, of my unofficial meetings of May….."

—⁓—

"Alice Nye was willing to tell me everything, right from the beginning. I have personally withheld some information from my superiors, out of respect for Ms. Nye's psychological state, and at her request. The threat to make public revelations was real, though never carried out; however, the material that Ms. Nye proposed to pass to the *Times* was innocuous, or rather, eccentric—of no intelligence value. Ms. Nye has written, and, as far as I know, continues to write, her own history of the final months of Cambodia's existence as a nation. Nye's account, included as an appendix, began with her brief captivity by cadres of the Khmer Rouge, apparently in January 1975. It was this period of incarceration in a KR camp south of Phnom Penh that precipitated Ms. Nye's breakdown, as described below. The following account contains material possibly related to Ms. Nye's psychological crisis—if I may call it that—as well as some personal revelations made to me during our interviews, material that she has asked me to keep private. I see no harm in this request; I have assented, and will honor her wishes in this regard.

"When I met Ms. Nye, approximately one week after her evacuation from the Embassy, she was in shock, or, rather, if I might use an awkward, but appropriate, figure of speech, she was nearly dead, not physically—she was in reasonably good health, but mentally she had passed to the world of the dead. This is an unusual comment, but truthful. It has been my lot to witness several mental breakdowns among agents, sources, and clients during twenty-six years of Agency service. I have seen individuals removed from high-stress situations, especially combat situations, whose stability was jeopardized by their experiences, but never before have I encountered anyone for whom the foundation of rational existence had so eroded. Had Ms. Nye been physically incapacitated her condition would have made more sense. Outwardly she wasn't unlike any of the other Embassy employees I interviewed. However, it soon became clear that the events she had witnessed, combined with what might best be termed her 'sensitive' nature—Ms. Nye appears to be unusually introspective and empathetic—led to her breakdown."

"Alice Nye was among over five hundred Americans and Cambodians extracted during Operation Eagle Pull as Phnom Penh fell to the Khmer Rouge. Some of the key Embassy personnel, including Ambassador Dean, arrived at Andrews Air Force Base in the middle of the night on April 16, 1975. Ms. Nye was in this group. A dozen agents were dispatched from Langley to meet the group, to see to their immediate needs—to arrange for medical care for some, and counseling for others—and, in the course of the following days, to debrief the evacuees. I was assigned a group that included Ms. Nye. She was calm and appeared to be fully in control of her emotions. We spoke briefly on the way from the airport to the accommodations that had been arranged for her in Arlington. When we next met, the following afternoon, I realized that I had misjudged her state of mind. What I had taken to be self-possession was a form of emotional self-defense. We spoke, during an initial meeting, held in her hotel room, for nine hours. At first I tape-recorded our conversation, then I took detailed notes, then rudimentary notes, finally, I simply listened. Later, after Ms. Nye had slept (she hadn't, she said, for over a week) and recovered her composure somewhat, she entrusted to me both autobiographical notes—personal matters with no bearing on the purview of my assignment—and detailed observations recorded during her time in-country. I have edited the personal matters but withheld them—the germane materials, written while in the service of the State Department, I have passed on to the appropriate agencies, primarily to the interagency group charged with debriefing all American citizens—Embassy personnel, reporters, Marine officers—who were the last to leave Cambodia—Democratic Kampuchea—and whose witness may prove invaluable as policies are being formulated in response to the twin debacles of April.

On a personal note—the sadness of Ms. Nye struck me as an apt counterpart to the sadness of our nation at this time of defeat and disillusionment." [End]

I have fabricated this alleged CIA account based on things that Alice told me during a long night of talking. She told me that she had suffered a "crisis" after she returned to the States, and that she "couldn't forget some of the things she had seen." Apparently there had been extensive debriefings, and, apart from the names of the agents, which she withheld and I made up, she gave me a reasonably full account of her "debriefing." She told me, "It was like intensive psychotherapy. It helped me to talk to someone, and both agents were surprisingly empathetic–older men, they'd seen a lot, and didn't judge me." Alice also told me that the agents with whom she had spoken had, "given her every courtesy" in light of her experiences in Cambodia.

A final note: G.K. Chesterton wrote someplace that believing in reality is itself an act of faith–but the impression of truth counts for a great deal when there is something at stake.

[2012] On Inauguration Day this exchange occurred between Alice and myself:

"You're married?"

"No." Her reply was emphatic.

"I only asked because of the ring."

"I was married. I haven't gotten around to taking off the ring."

"Did he work at the Embassy?"

"No. He was my teacher in college. It's a long story. I don't think I'll tell you about it."

"That's fine with me."

And it was fine, because it wasn't Alice's marriage that I was interested in talking about. We had only a short time, that was clear, and it was Cambodia I wanted to speak about. I said that we never met again, or spoke. And that is true, but Alice did send me a statement, an affidavit I think you could call it. She mailed it from Hammonton to the Van Pelt, and since she only knew my first name she wrote on the envelope—"Please deliver to Wallace, the gentleman with the injured leg"—an odd and impulsive thing to do. The circulation librarians, who didn't know me from Adam, stuck the envelope in a cubby-hold in their office and forgot about it. You couldn't blame them. I didn't have a library card, and I wasn't a student, and only a few of them knew my name. There were other gentlemen with bad legs, mostly older, who used the library, so why should they think of me? One day in early spring I was making some photocopies in the main lobby, right in front of the check-out station, leaning on my cane and probably appearing uncommonly weary, when one of the librarians came over to me with an envelope. She asked me if I knew who Alice Nye was and I told her that I did know her, though not well. She apologized for forgetting about the envelope, but she said it seemed *off* to her—that was the word she used, 'off'—the idea that someone would address mail to the patron of a university library, and a guest at that. But I was the wounded man in question, no doubt, and since librarians are fastidious people, she wanted to make sure the delivery was made. The affidavit was a kind of personal statement, the sort of thing you might write as part of an application for a grant or a job. The bare facts of her life, with no judgments attached —and this part of her existence was of no concern to me. Later on however, when I wanted to write some things down about what she had told me, and also when I wanted to recall that particular day, I reread her "Notes on My Failures" as she styled it. The following pages, ones in which I have no part, are adapted, or quoted, from these notes.

It appears that her husband was a decent man, but one who had no past, no sentimental connections to anyone, no sense of tradition, and was the victim of Alice's romantic yearning for a life that existed only in her imagination. The life she had led with her mother and father had been one of mutual regard and real affection unencumbered by the expectations that ruin most relationships. Later on, perhaps hoping to recover her past, Alice fell in love with, or imagined herself in love with Philip Turley. Rather quickly, and for what appear to be political reasons, she came to feel alienated from him—sorry, that's a terrible word to use, so let's say that she felt disaffected and leave it at that—and after a little over a year of marriage, she abandoned him for another life, one not empty of delusions. Finally, long after they were divorced, decades perhaps, she loved him again—this time with a purity and ferocity that might have mattered before, but which was by then self-destructive. I find this sort of analysis tedious and have been surprised by my willingness to indulge in such fanciful speculation. I admit to a fascination with this woman I hardly knew. Her story has come to lodge itself in my mind in a baffling way. This happens to lonely people. They—that is, I—fix on someone who appears to be empathetic, but who isn't at all interested, who is only polite or solicitous, yet the power of illusion is so great that the lonely person—and that would be me—concocts a life story out of someone's illusory interest. Lonely people are dangerous to themselves, but they are more dangerous to innocent bystanders who make the mistake of being kind to them.

<hr>

Alice took Turley's "Introduction to Philosophy" and then his seminar on "Theories of Mind." The topic didn't interest her, but the opportunity to hear more of Turley's ideas on a range of issues, or maybe just to be around someone whose life seemed settled and coherent, drew her in.

She was a dutiful student, not brilliant, but hard working and bright enough to figure things out. Alice never missed any classes and seldom failed to pay attention. She lived alone, in a dull dorm room, and didn't have many friends—she missed her family, her mother most of all, and didn't like the city. Washington seemed to Alice an unnatural place, everyone crammed into a few square miles, palaces of the government and mansions of the rich on one side of town and squalid slums on the other. Jim Crow was alive and well in Washington, and though she had little experience with black people, Alice was embarrassed by the poverty that existed a block from the grandiose capitol building, with its gilded murals and aristocratic chambers.

Alice had a scholarship, but college was expensive, and her parents had borrowed a little money to give her the education they hadn't had. The weight of this debt deepened Alice's commitment to learning. She filled her room with books from the library and from the cheap second-hand shops along Wisconsin Avenue. She read everything that came her way, and searched out obscure writers her professors mentioned in class. She studied French and German, wrote poems and long research papers, spending sleepless nights drinking coffee and filling index cards with random facts. It dawned on Alice that while the world outside of Mullica wasn't quite real to her, she could make up a version of it in her tiny room at Georgetown. The room was her brain, the books and papers ideas, or facts that could become ideas, a form of power that was benign and private, a power that could transform her not into someone else, but into who she had been all along.

On the third day at home after her mother's death, after a sleepless night, Alice borrowed her father's car and drove to the shore. The beach had never appealed to Alice, the open space made her dizzy and the vastness of the ocean felt crushing. A verse from Paul Eluard came to her as she parked her car and walked toward the shore—"There is another world/but it is in this one." She couldn't tell if the poet was offering hope or counseling despair, but at just that moment, with the sun passing weakly through the thick clouds and the damp air sweeping her hair into her face, Alice felt that no world could contain her sadness, and that she might as well walk straight out into the frigid waves. But she didn't. Instead she walked to the point where ridges of white foam collected on the black sand and spent a long time emptying her mind and staring into the nothing that is the winter ocean.

She said to me, "I was in terrible pain when my mother died, and the feeling of emptiness brought back the other great trauma of my life. I acted strangely, and did things that were wholly out of character. Did you ever find your-self standing aside from all your inhibitions, from the things you believe to be most important—you must have, since you went through something that never relinquishes its hold, from war and all of the moral chaos that goes with it. Then you know what I was like for many years—just holding on to what I had salvaged of myself. And then I made a life again, and it held up, it sustained me -- until my mother died. That doesn't excuse some things I did, but then I don't believe in or ask for forgiveness."

It was raining hard on the day that Alice and Philip became lovers. They collided like blind animals—that sounded about right to Alice. Volition, forethought, weighing of consequences, all their critical faculties had been suspended.

From the seminar room the dozen students could look south over Key Bridge and the churning Potomac River. There was the skyline of Arlington, glass towers housing the think tanks of the opposition—in that year the Democrats—reporters for newsmagazines, and the other institutions that surrounded the capital like weeds, or at least this was what Alice thought as she let her mind drift from her teacher's remarks on Descartes, articulated with a slow deliberate cadence designed to imitate the bricking of a wall, laying in each proposition carefully, waiting for objections, indeed welcoming objections that never came, all the students copying down each simple sentence, subject, predicate, pause—Turley smoked a pipe and constantly fiddled with it, tamping and lighting and relighting tobacco that smelled to Alice like vanilla-fudge—*and so, and yet, and then*. Philosophy seemed pointless to Alice, but in the same way that string quartets or Rothko murals were pointless— their irrelevance served to illuminate the deeper emptiness of everything else, the waste of time that was ordinary life. Having understood this, Alice realized that she had potential as a philosopher.

Jets bound for National Airport would swoop along the Potomac perilously close to the treetops and apartment houses, the deep roar blending with evening traffic already locked onto the bridge as the frantic emptying of the city began. The white people who worked for the government dreaded being trapped in the city that was full of black people. It was crude to say, but Washington was material evidence that racism would never end—fight or flee, but never coexist.

Alice thought that Georgetown seemed an unlikely spot for a university, a little indefensible hill surrounded by commerce, politics, and slums. Now dreamy, seduced by the romance of ideas, rich talk, conversation as warm as home, at home was what she felt, comfortable, participating in the great unending enterprise of truth. With her colleagues Alice was unfolding the past by concentrating for hours on the words of a dozen books, the same books, Alice knew, that had been poured over by millions who had come before, ideas opening like flowers, perhaps too fertile, too divorced from anything she was familiar with, ideas leading to some higher understanding The metaphor was irresistible, she was transcending her own life—out of the cave, into the light. Until, as it transpired, she vanished into thin air.

When she came back to the room Turley was smiling in her direction.

"Been away for a bit, have you?"

"Sorry. It's the rain, the lights. Looking out there at the evening is hypnotic."

The other members of the class tried laughing, not sure if laughter was permissible. Turley wasn't touchy, but he was serious.

Some pipe banging on the ashtray. Professor Turley looks at the class warmly, takes them all in, sweeps them up in the way good teachers sometimes do, implying that, no matter what, they are all in this together. Nothing is easier than feeling affection when there is no cost.

"She's right of course. The lights on the bridge draw us in. Raw sense data. Let's read this next part together shall we? Alice, would you? At the top of 21?"

Later on, after she and Philip knew each other intimately, after they had moved in together, "merged their libraries" as he had put it, he would read to Alice the lines from Petrarch, *"When I first realized/The transfiguration of my person,"* he taught her the Italian, read to her whole of the twenty-third song to Laura, skipping over the line *"my sorrow being invisible,"* running quickly through the poet's sadness to linger on the stanzas that show love as inevitable—*"God makes love where he will"*—love which lifts one above oneself, above the world itself. It was that moment in the seminar room, Philip said, that caused him to recall the lines from Petrarch that he had memorized in high school, not understanding what they entailed, but wanting the sentiments to live in him until such time as he would feel their power.

Alice read: *From these considerations I am beginning to know a little better what I am. But it still seems (and I cannot resist believing) that corporeal things–whose images are formed by thought, and which the senses themselves examine–are much more distinctly known than this mysterious 'I' which does not fall within the imagination.*

Turley finished the thought for her, "My mind loves to wander and does not yet permit itself to be restricted within the confines of truth."

He was quiet for a moment, and then a woman sitting next to Alice said, "So odd, to speak of the mind as if it were in conversation with itself about the things it knows or doesn't know, like a pet left off the leash."

Turley was looking at Alice and did not respond. Alice was concentrating on her book. Other students took up the argument, if that was what it was. Turley listened, lit his pipe, and then explained mind-body dualism, as Descartes had understood it. The class ended soon afterwards, but, as she knew she would, Alice remained behind, casually packing up her books, waiting for an invitation that seemed inevitable.

Turley hadn't moved. When the other students were gone, he said, "I don't mind when you leave us Alice, but when you return the class improves."

"I'm sorry. It's rude of me." She looked at him and shrugged.

"Let's go for coffee. I think things will work out."

Alice later remembered thinking that this was an ambiguous promise, coming from one who was ordinarily so precise.

<hr>

Philip was a timid lover, and, though older and more educated, he was eager to have someone take charge of him. He lacked the will to dominate, as if like one of Kant's moral beings he followed rules of behavior, imperatives of acting, without thinking and without volition. Alice seduced him soon after their first evenings spent together. She suggested what, and when, and she led him to bed as if he were a boy. Alice had no plans for their relationship, no desire to make a few casual hours of sex and conversation more than what it was—another part of her education. Not one to learn only from books, Alice had a desire to learn, as with all of her senses, to come more fully alive in the world that had now opened itself to her. As for Philip, it may have occurred to him that he was behaving like one of Descartes candles—melting in the fire, assuming another shape altogether. Then again, Alice was a beautiful young woman, and he wasn't a fool.

Not entirely anyway.

Philip pretended that his head ruled his heart, but Alice's body convinced him with the force of an incontrovertible logical proof that reason was of no use. This was the way the mind-body problem had always been resolved, with the mind forgotten in the face of the body's yearning. Philip had a sense of humor about himself. He saw that he was hopeless, and he didn't resist the feelings that hopelessness engendered. If this be folly, he thought, well then, so be it.

He wanted Alice to move in with him at once, but she said no, it wasn't wise to rush into anything, and he had his followers to think of; she had said "disciples" at first, trying to be witty, but the word stung Philip and she regretted using it.

"They're hardly that," he said.

"You know what I mean. You're popular. People love to drop in, to talk with you, to drink your beer. It's going to be awkward for me to be living with you. There's got to be a rule about that at a Catholic school."

"I'm sure there is one, but that's a matter of no concern. We can be discreet."

"I don't think that's possible Philip. People who are sleeping together are never discreet."

They were in his office having this conversation. He stood up and closed the door, and then he kissed her.

⁓

Intimacy requires confession, or at least the fashioning of a story that casts one in an attractive light. Later, one's guard goes up, and truth-telling loses its charm. Alice and Philip swapped stories over the course of a few weeks in the winter and early spring of their relationship. Alice was reticent; Philip was not.

Philip told her that he came from a dysfunctional family, but everyone did. It turned out that the problems he faced growing up were common, but weren't often spoken about until the sixties. His father drank too much, and his mother, a gentle woman, endured his abuse. An only child, Philip did his best to absent himself from an unhappy home. He was bookish and withdrawn. His father accused Philip of being "queer," and Philip hated his father with a passion that poisoned all of the other relationships in his life. When his father died of liver cancer, Philip felt nothing.

Like Alice, Philip had succumbed to a rich interior life. He had been unhappy; she had been isolated, though not alone and certainly not unloved. If irony is the recognition that no one way of thinking can ever be correct, then Philip and Alice were made for each other, for neither of them was able to embrace the world they grew up in—admitting this fact about herself took Alice many years; for Philip, discontentment was a given. Their attraction was enriched by their loneliness. "What do we do next?" was an important question for Philip. In other words, how should we live? Alice made him forget that the answers to such questions matter.

131

Not that reflection was pointless, but that the physical being of someone else can cancel our doubts and allow us merely to be. Maybe he mistook gratitude for love. It happens.

Alice moved into his house, shared his bed, and took turns cooking the elaborate meals that neither one cared about, but that seemed a mandatory part of academic life. They had company, and let it be known that second- and third-order friends were welcome to join in the communal Friday dinners that became notorious, boisterous social events. Friends of friends invited community organizers, untalented poets and singers, low-level bureaucrats, activists of all persuasions, pastors of marginal churches, gay and straight and bisexual artists, the great melting pot that was Washington, D.C. in the early 1970's came and broke bread in Philip and Alice's Georgetown house—it was exhilarating to be around them in those early days, to listen to the talk, the good-natured and acerbic and angry arguments, as if they were residing in the great salons of Madame de Stäel or Marie Thérèse Geoffrin. By early spring, two months after they had started to share their lives, Philip and Alice found themselves at the center of a society that was charged by politics, by outrage at the events unfolding in the first years of the new decade—the War of course, but also the coarsening of civil life.

Admiration and love, history and forgetting, body and mind. Alice spent years working through the dichotomies of her life, finding out that the ways in which all the seemingly opposite forces of her existence blended into a great confusion.

Back at home, four days after her return, with the wound of her mother's death still fresh, Alice sat with her father. They spoke quietly until they ran out of things to say. Then they sat without speaking, Bob in his recliner, staring out the window. The room, the family den, was seedy and tattered. The cheap carpet was worn in two tight semicircles running toward the kitchen and the bathroom. The bookshelves, crammed with paperbacks, knickknacks and the debris of life—snow globes from their trip to Maine, Kodak prints faded to sepia and curled into tight cylinders, coffee cups stuffed with broken pens, souvenir matchbooks from Cape May and Philadelphia—places Alice couldn't recall having ever visited—"feather pennies" and coins of real silver and Eisenhower dimes that Bob believed would someday be worth a fortune—in other words, the junk of ordinary life, objects that meant enough to save but whose purpose was now inscrutable. They sat, father and daughter, each battered by the finality of their loss, each turning over in the course of a gray afternoon a host of memories, of quiet evenings sitting at the kitchen table, of walks in the pitch pine forest, of fishing trips to Long Beach Island. What else was there to think about but the residue of a life that once seemed as if it would go on forever? At one point Alice made her father a sandwich. He took it in his oversized hand but put it down at once, as though eating would be a violation of his duty to mourn his wife. Alice went to the book shelves and picked out a collection of poems that her mother had loved.

She said to her father, as quietly as she could, "Listen to

this. It's was one of Mom's favorite poems," and then she read the poem without inflection, ignoring the cadences and the end stops—she rushed to the end so that she wouldn't tear up.

> *It is a cold and snowy night. The main street is deserted.*
> *The only things moving are swirls of snow.*
> *As I lift the mailbox door, I feel its cold iron.*
> *There is a privacy I love in this snowy night.*
> *Driving around, I will waste more time.*

"You're right, your mother loved that poem. Did I ever tell you we saw Bly read?"

"No. Where was that?"

"At Montclair State. You were already in college. I think, 1967 or '68. He wore a serape and had long blond hair. I think your mother had a crush on him. There weren't many people, and he was very kind. He read and then talked about his life in Minnesota. And afterwards we had coffee and the students surrounded him and your mother went up and said hello. It was the only poetry reading I ever went to in my life, and I'm sorry for that. I liked him, and I liked the simple words about winter and the country. You think 'How could it be so easy to make a poem?' But you know that it isn't easy at all. First you have to feel things. You mother felt things in that way."

"Yes. And she said things to us that were like poems. Do you remember how she would say that the gentians grew in the fire so that the red of their petals would glow in the night? And it was true. The fires would open the ground up for the flowers. And in the dimmest light they looked like bits of flame."

***

Alice and Philip married on the equinox in the disastrous spring of 1970. Alice thought she could finish school and go to work. She would major in politics or international relations, help Philip with his research, maintain a household—she would be her mother and he would be—not her father, that wasn't possible, but a man like him, self-reliant and dedicated to her. She would get a job at the State Department or at a think tank, specializing in Southeast Asia. They would travel and, eventually, have children. Not everyone had yet given up on the roles they had been taught to play. Bohemianism wasn't the American way. Educated men and women wanted the war to end, for Nixon to be voted out of office, for the Great Society to heal the wounds of inequality, for Civil Rights to be extended to the benighted South; but these same men and women also wanted jobs and houses and kids. They weren't turning their back on middle class life, just smoothing out its rough edges. Alice thought of herself at this stage in her life as 'liberal,' and that was, in her mind, the best thing one could be.

The problem was that history caught up with them, or at least it waylaid Alice from her dreamy commitment to a normal life. History—as in the collapse of the tissue of lies that was the 'American Way of Life'. In the paddies of South Vietnam, in the streets of Chicago, in the burning cities of the Northeast, in the visceral images of dead boys and their dead enemies lying on tarmacs at Lakehurst and

Cam Ranh Air Base, in the anger of workers and college kids and women at a political process that shut them out. This was what Alice came to see as the way it was—the great lie exposed at last.

Philip and Alice were happy for a shorter time than Alice thought possible. Their social life continued, the visitors still came, though less often and with less enthusiasm. Many of Turley's female admirers dropped away, disappointed in their failure to fill the place now so ingenuously occupied by an upstart undergraduate—pretty enough, but shallow. The men still came, and the conversations were fine, but, in light of the moment, the "grave crisis" as everyone referred to the expansion of the War, the daily sense that anything might happen, many passionate students of philosophy and history found their older interests giving way to passionate politics. The momentum of this change had been building for years—since 1963 said some; for others, since the widening of the War; others thought the turning point had come much earlier—under Truman, with the National Security Act and the creation of a permanent state of conflict. Arguments on this point could become theological in their niceties. Alice never paid any attention to them. A seismic shift in her world had come when she visited Cambodia. Now, with that neutral country embroiled in Nixon and Kissinger's secret plotting, everything changed. Most people only become political when the issues are personal. That was true of Alice. She felt the bombing in her blood and bones.

"I've been wasting my time," she told her husband, and this remark stung Philip, who remained committed to his work.

"What's the point of these abstractions," she would say, or "how can we afford the luxury of philosophy at a time like this?"

And Philip would reply that now, more than ever, was when reflection and philosophy were required.

"Reflection is complicity."

"Jesus Alice, you sound like a bumper sticker. Where do you get this stuff? I'm teaching people how to think. Someday they might run the world. You know the argument. Education is the one place in life where profits and losses don't matter, where there's no bottom line. Every minute of learning, whatever the learning is about, is an investment in a decent future for everyone. How could it be otherwise? Ignorance is cruelty. Think of *suttee*. Think of the bigotries of history. Don't make yourself a force for ignorance by memorizing slogans."

"That was before. Everything is different now. We're bombing a neutral country. You have to *act*. The goals you believe in are noble, but we're talking about saving lives. I don't disagree with you, but think about what it means to say to people who are being bombed, 'you have to consider the future.' They don't have a future. Surely you understand that."

Philip looked at Alice as if for the first time.

"I am *acting*." He spat the word. He hated the idea that a person's life could be reduced to make believe. "And I hate to have to tell you this, but the good old US of A has been bombing innocent people since the Spanish-American War. And before that, we executed them in more mundane ways. Ever hear of Sand Creek? Wounded Knee? That's where an education comes in handy—you can put things into perspective." He hated to talk to his wife in this way, to hector her with facts. He yearned to take her in his arms as he had on those afternoons a year before. But there was something amiss in him as well, some anger he hadn't realized he felt. The 'movement,' as it was styled by his students, was deeply anti-intellectual; in fact, the handful of Georgetown SDS members, the Black Nationalists, the feminists all agreed that reason was the monster that had given birth to the bomb and to imperialism and to rapacious corporate capitalism. Reason, the liberator of the human spirit, was now being excoriated by people who were paying thousands of dollars to study the fruits of the human intellect. *This* was madness.

"Don't condescend to me Philip. I know something about history. Not as much as you, but something. The bombs we're dropping on Cambodia and North Vietnam aren't some abstract lesson in moral philosophy. Come on Philip. You aren't some cold-hearted intellectual. You feel things deeply. Don't you see how important it is that we stop this cruelty now?"

Alice's tone was calm and, he knew, deeply felt. It hurt Philip to think that his wife—his wife!—would have to remind him that he wasn't unfeeling. But now he was angry. "And how *are* we going to stop it? Are *we* going to burn ourselves alive in front of the White House? Because if that's your plan, count me out."

"Burn myself? What a terrible, mocking thing to say. You know that people *have* burned themselves, Buddhists in South Vietnam and now in Cambodia. This should tell you how deeply they feel. And we need to feel something as well."

"You think I don't? You think I'm not disgusted with what is being done in my name? But that isn't a reason to renounce everything you believe in, everything that's good in our lives."

"What's good in our lives is different now."

Did Alice say this? Why not? Many people did just then. The world had become very old, or perhaps it had ended, and anyone who was paying attention felt it.

At home, a day after Alice had visited the beach, her father had a heart attack. She was making coffee in the kitchen and heard a noise from the other side of the house. Bob was lying on the floor in the bathroom, panicked, holding his chest. His face was contorted with pain. Alice ran into the bedroom and called 911. She rubbed his chest and legs and spoke gently to him—he was breathing in short, rapid gasps, but he said he was all right—he kept saying it over and over, that he was fine, as if saying so would make it true. Before the ambulance arrived he could sit up with his back against the toilet. His color was returning, but he was trembling. When the paramedics arrived they asked Bob some questions, then they put him on a gurney and rolled him out to the ambulance. Alice rode with her father to the hospital. He was coherent, but the brightness of his eyes, his trembling hands, worried her. At the regional medical center in Hammonton he was given an EKG. The doctors weren't in much of a hurry, and Alice began to think that the crisis had passed. A young doctor whose name tag said "Lassiter" told Alice that her father had suffered a mild heart attack, but that tests would have to be done for a better diagnosis.

"Will he live?" Alice felt stupid asking the question, but what other question was there?

"He should be fine. We don't know for sure what the cause of his chest pains was—there are several possibilities. After we ascertain the cause precisely, we can undertake a therapy. Drugs or perhaps surgery. It's too soon to tell."

"Can I see him?"

"Just for a few minutes."

In the IC unit, Alice's father was surrounded by machines with digital readouts, information that frightened Alice, perhaps because of its clarity, the terrible certainty of the body. Bob was asleep, or unconscious—there is a difference, and Alice saw what it was just then. She touched her father's hand, said something under her breath, and left.

On April 30th, President Nixon went on television to explain the widening of the war. The *sanctuaries*—Alice detested this word—*interdiction, repressing fire, incursion, search and destroy*—words and concepts that no one had known a week before now dominated conversation. Alice went to school but stopped going to class. She joined a group that was reading the works of Bernard Fall. She joined SDS, which meant nothing. You went to meetings which went on nonstop and consisted in erudite arguments on the finer points of revolutionary theory. More importantly, she joined the Provisional Committee Against the War—"provisional," she supposed, because not everyone got along or agreed on strategy, or even knew what the word "strategy" meant—in any case she passed her days with students who wrote and distributed broadsides, pamphlets, and handouts for the "working class" of Georgetown, if there were such a thing. She chaired a Solidarity Committee with the goal of broadening understanding of Southeast Asia as a whole, work she felt uniquely qualified for, but which few activists supported—too intellectual they said, or a diversion from the "main work." Much of the irony that she came to feel about her involvement didn't exist until later, when, with the withdrawal of the troops and the growing irrelevance of the draft, most students grew bored with the war. It turns out, she said later, that the anti-war movement was like many other things in America, basically a way of covering one's ass. Some of the high-minded protests were sincere, but quite a lot of activism turned on the anger of those who were used to doing as they pleased and who were terrified that they too might have to fight.

She sold her textbooks back to the bookstore. She was done with philosophy and English literature and anthropology—done for good, or so she said. Within weeks of Nixon's bland announcement that Cambodia was being bombed to interdict the movement of NVA troops and supplies to the South, Alice could cite the Geneva Accords by heart and was quoting Mao, Ho, and Che. Two days after the President's speech, she was arrested for chaining herself to the front of the White House gate and had to spend a night in the Metropolitan Detention Center.

Philip wasn't impressed. He was disdainful of the protesters, not because he disagreed with their politics, but because he thought their "gestures" were futile.

"That's an absurd word to use. They aren't *gestures*," Alice insisted.

"A gesture is symbolic. It has no substance. No causal implications."

"Causal implications? My God, Philip, you sound like an idiot. Our country is bombing innocent people in our name and you're making logical distinctions?"

"Then games. You're playing games, enacting rituals of protest."

"Bullshit. In that regard, everything is a game. Marriage, love, politics, teaching. They're all rituals, Philip. But some rituals matter more than others. You know that."

"I'm being honest. Action that leads to nothing is empty. Cries of anguish that become ritualized, daily marches and protests, they don't change anything. Deep change comes from doing your duty, your job."

"*Jati.* Caste. That's what you're describing. Preserve the institutions at all costs. What we are saying is that the institutions have betrayed us. It's time for them to be thrown over. Ending the war isn't enough. The structure of the war machine will just find another conflict."

"Well my love, good luck. I'm going to work. I guess I'm part of the problem."

And so it went, passion meeting detachment, with neither Philip nor Alice giving an inch. The argument was probably about something else.

Philip counseled his students to keep at their school work, graduate and change the system from within. Formerly an outsider, Philip now found himself beleaguered on all sides—he sounded staid compared to his more progressive colleagues, like a Jesuit—though many of the younger priests had also joined the protestors—and so he was nearly alone, part of a small group of the "reactionary" faculty. In one class, in the midst of a lecture on Hobbes, a bearded young man who might not even have been a student stood up and began to shout "pig" and "collaborator" at Philip. Most of the students in the class cheered the interloper and many walked out. Those who remained behind were, Philip knew, worried about their grades. He was stunned. Never had he been interrupted or spoken to with disrespect; he gathered up his notes and went home. When he told Alice about the episode she seemed gratified, as if he was getting what he deserved.

After this confrontation, Philip elected to become the spokesman for opposition to the protests, especially the massive demonstrations that began on May Day. A reporter heard about his role and interviewed Philip for a sidebar—"Noted Georgetown Scholar Defies Campus Radicals." Philip expressed his viewpoint coolly, with detachment—the primacy of Reason, the tradition of civil discourse, Madison's views in *Federalist Ten*, Thoreau of course, also Locke on Civil Society and Rawls and, heaven help him, Aquinas' view of natural law—it was an urbane and reasoned reply to what Philip saw as a tawdry interruption in the Great Tradition—he even quoted Plato's view that dialectic led invariably to truth. The reaction to all of this high thinking was of course outrage, not only from the core of the campus radical movement—which was by no means large—but by nearly everyone. Philip came off as cold-blooded, detached to the point of disinterest in the visceral realities of war and its consequences. He was embarrassed by his tone, by his abstract pronouncements—the arrogance!—but he had to stand by what he said because, in truth, it was what he believed. There were two forces at work in the world—everyone knew this was so—the force of light and thought and sweet reason and only they stood against the darkness of passion and irrationality. Who was he kidding? And, worse, when you came right down to it what *was* the difference between conniving Kissinger and lying Nixon and a buffoon like Abby Hoffman? The truth was that the war—the War—wasn't about the conflict in Southeast Asia but about the young versus the old, the uptight Establishment Republican money machine—"menopausal white men"—and hipsters who protested so that they could hook up, get stoned, and screw some flower child. The whole mess was reducible to a simple Freudian paradigm—to hatred of the Father, to the unleashing of the libido (a development that Philip wholly supported, both as a scholar and as a man), to the fundamental American dialectic of Puritan Elder versus capitalist libertine. In Philip's eyes the young were the children of privilege—ten grand to attend Georgetown for a year!—kids who'd grown up in the neurotic, uptight 50s, the spawn of the Great War, spoiled middle-class kids who were weaned on television shows that celebrated an unprecedented prosperity and claustrophobic bourgeois families—*Father Knows Best* until the shit hits the fan, until pot and rock and a bunch of lying politicians revealed the black heart of American virtue. Philip knew the story himself; hell, he'd lived it. There was always some lie festering at the heart of the American story—the providential God, the equal playing field, the nuclear family, the nation committed to equality and opportunity. Philip put away the illusions one by one as he grew up. First he gave up the church, then his family, then his country, then, he supposed, he gave up on himself. The whole is the sum of its parts—what else could it be? And if the whole story was fetid with lies, and if he, in his heart of hearts, still clung to them in some desperate way, then what was he but a liar? And so, in the spring of 1970, with the tattered banners torn down at last, Philip lied about his feelings—and his feelings were easy to lie about since, as he knew, they were dead in him. At least McNamara believed in bombing innocent people. Philip neither believed nor disbelieved in much of anything.

As the cherry blossoms wilted and filled the Tidal Basin with their pink corpses, Philip lost his bearings. He said things that he knew were untrue. He betrayed his heart, and that was bad, but what was worse was his betrayal of his only faith—his faith in reason. That it kills the heart makes betrayal evil; that it kills the intellect makes it fatal.

Rather than think much about what he was saying, he took to berating his wife.

"Who cares if you spend a night in jail? Nixon? Don't kid yourself Alice, the war's going to end when the generals say it will end, and even if you were to cut out your heart in Lafayette Square no one would care. That's what power is about. Power is the ability to create indifference. Chaining yourself to the White House? What's that supposed to accomplish?"

"We didn't chain ourselves. We held onto the bars. You ever see that fucking place? Here we are down the street from Fort Nixon and we never looked at the thing—it's scary. It isn't in the world. They can't see us. We have to make them pay attention."

"They won't. Believe me Alice, they won't. 'The whole world is watching?' My ass it is. The only thing they're watching is *Johnny Carson*."

—⁓—

One by one, things were falling away. It seemed odd to Alice that people accumulated objects and were gratified, thinking that possessions gave them solidity and wedded them to the world, but they didn't notice what they lost, day after day, how one thing after another is lost, imperceptibly. People you love die, and with them you die yourself—inch by inch. Alice had made a close study of Buddhist thought at Georgetown, and during the time she lived in Cambodia she had immersed herself in Theravada Buddhism. She understood that the world which appears to us to be dense with meaning is illusionary, and that it is folly to cling to material things—*skanda*, the aggregates of materiality that bind us to the world must be loosened if we are to be free. And yet while Alice came to understand this view, to accept it with her western mind—one given to thinking in ways that reinforced the deep attachments she felt to things— when it came to her own life she could not bear to let go of the things she loved. Her parents most of all, her belief in politics, her conviction that ideas mattered. And now

146

the last remaining pillars of her life were being taken away from her.

Her father didn't die, but he didn't live either. It turned out that he hadn't had a pulmonary embolism—it was something else, but no one was quite sure what. The doctors called it a 'trauma' which Alice kept hearing as 'drama,' as if her father had staged his own near-dying. The problem was that health had become another victim of America's fixation on individualism—the admitting nurse asked Alice dozens of questions about her father's "lifestyle," a word Bob wouldn't have understood. Did he smoke? Use drugs? Did he drink and, if so, how much? Did he eat red meat?

"I don't know," Alice had told the nurse, "are squirrels red meat?"

This question elicited stony silence. Alice filled it by saying what was on her mind.

"What difference does it make if my father drank beer or smoked or ate too many hot dogs? He's here now, and ill, just like you and I will be one day. So let's not waste a lot of time on his 'lifestyle.'"

Alice stayed in the hospital overnight, and the next day a different doctor told her that her father had an arterial blockage that would require angioplasty. The doctor was in a hurry, but answered most of Alice's questions. She didn't ask if her father would be all right; she was assuming he would be, just as she was assuming he needed surgery and a stent and months of recovery—what else could she do? The hospital stay alone would bankrupt her and her father; his paltry medical plan wouldn't pay for half the costs of the procedure, so as an indigent patient in a public hospital, Bob had to take what he got—no flying off to the Mayo Clinic for a second opinion.

Alice went home for a night's sleep. She lay awake for hours and then drifted into a sequence of nightmares that conflated certain indelibly-etched scenes from Cambodia with her father's clogged arteries and her husband's angry cries—then, half-asleep, she showered and ate a meal and put on fresh clothes.

Heart surgery had an innocent ring to it, as if the patient had embraced his fate with tranquility. The thought of her father opened up like a Francis Bacon painting—she couldn't get the image out of her mind—was insupportable to Alice—she read poetry and Agatha Christie to drive the demons of her own imagination away. After five hours the doctor came out with good and bad news. Bob would live, but he would be incapacitated for some time. His recovery would be slow. Apparently Alice's father hadn't been taking care of himself. There was irreparable damage to the heart. Was there someone to care for him? His wife? Could he afford a nurse?

Alice heard the questions but their import didn't register. Of course she knew that she would care for her father. And why not, she wasn't doing anything else. The thought of doing so depressed her and she wasn't sure why. She loved her father, but from a distance. The intimacy of nursing him made her uneasy.

"Will he ever recover?"

"That depends on what you mean by 'recover'," said the doctor.

"By 'recover' I mean be his old self, more or less."

"In that case the answer is maybe, more or less."

The doctor's accent had a pleasant lilt, as if he was enjoying the ambiguities of English and pleased by his ability to express them.

"I see. Do you think that an untrained person like me could provide the care he needs?"

"I don't see why not. Your father will be able to do most things, but he will be weak for several months. It will be critical that he take his medications. He can't drive or clean house or go to the market. We will monitor his progress and before long he should be able to do more for himself."

"When can he go home?"

"Not for a while yet. Several days, maybe longer. We'll know soon."

"We always do, don't we?"

Alice watched her father sleep, emptying her mind. She remembered how to forget, and decided now was a good time to do so. Then, after telling the nurse she would return in a day or two, she went back to the home of her parents, packed a few things, and returned to Philadelphia.

⸺⁓⸺

A few days after the May Day demonstrations, Nixon and Kissinger escalated the bombing. Alice watched the surreal images of Vietnam burning. The War—now officially a proper noun—was a fire behind her eyes, an ache that wouldn't go away. In Alice's nightmares the flutter of helicopter blades blended with silent screams of burning 'hooches'—the word set Alice's teeth on edge, a word that turned a home into an disposable afterthought—GIs were pictured in *Life*—as if the world could bear any more irony—flicking their Zippos and setting fire to grass roofs. Feeling nearly mad, Alice gave up her studies and took up *Sutta Pitaka* and Pure Land texts translated from Pali, hallucinogenic books that failed to sooth her aching heart. There is nothing worse than empathy in wartime—Alice could see the villages burning—she could see little else. She went to a poetry reading that featured Allen Ginsburg, a wild hairy shaman-poet who danced and chanted to the lugubrious heaves of a strange accordion pumped in metronomic sighs by a man dressed in a loincloth. Alice got high before the reading and went home with a guy she'd sat next to—a graduate student in English who said he'd been in Vietnam—maybe he had been. She'd lost control of her feelings. Afterwards she felt guilty, but not as much as she thought she should.

The U.S. Navy mined Haiphong Harbor. B-52s the size of islands floated above the green seas of North Vietnam, dropping incendiary devices—gray canisters toppling awkwardly onto the distant earth. After a moment, in the bland flickering TV image—a swirl of electrons beamed half-way around the world—the green landscape would erupt into flames, as the Agent Orange or white phosphorus rained down on the Ho Chi Minh trail, on North Vietnam, on Cambodia. Philip watched with Alice. She cried quietly; he comforted her, but didn't say much. One view, Philip's, was that there was nothing to say, that words were inadequate to capture certain situations, that, once again, words failed us, and that understanding would come later on, in the cool sessions of debriefing undertaken by historians and philosophers. Another view, Alice's, was that you had to talk about those tumbling bombs all day and all night, you had to speak about it non-stop or go mad, you had to wrap the putrid reality of it in a cloud of words so thick that it would fit into the vast horror of human experience—"it" being not only the images of falling cylinders of dioxin-laced fire, but also the things you might allow yourself to imagine if you didn't keep talking. Like: what the fuck happened to the people underneath those bursts of flame?

A few days after the B-52s, Alice was arrested again, spending two nights in jail. She was put on probation. In late May, during daily protests on the Mall, she was tear-gassed and pounded on the forearms and shoulders by a federal marshal. A week later she and a few comrades were pelted with eggs by a group of men and women waving American flags and pictures of Nixon. She came home late and sometimes didn't come home at all. She went home with men and sometimes with women. She had sex with them or she didn't—the point was to keep talking, to stay angry, and to not grow indifferent. A person she met turned her on to speed and she was able to stop eating and sleeping. Sleeping was out of the question. She and Philip fought when they saw each other, which wasn't often. The war, Philip thought, had come home, just as the protestors wanted.

"Politics is bad enough, a sham, a lie, but what you're doing is worse. It's masturbation, self-regard of the cheapest kind. You and your phony friends, the drugs. Christ Alice, six months ago you were intelligent."

"And I'm stupid now?"

"No. I'm saying you've stopped thinking. It's what they want. They want people to rush into the streets where they can be controlled. Think about it. What changes things? Ideas matter Alice, not getting beat up by cops."

"That's glib Philip. What 'ideas' are you talking about? This is about power nothing else. And being willing to stop the machine."

"Oh fuck, Alice, listen to yourself. That's idiotic. 'Stop the machine.' Jesus Christ."

"Is it? What's dropping napalm on those people Philip? Would that be the ideas you love so much? Talk about masturbation—that's all you academics do. The machine is the Pentagon. They have to see that we won't just go along with the War. It's that simple."

"Well, good luck Alice. And enjoy the drugs and the screwing around while you're at it."

This remark stopped Alice cold.

"What? You think I'm stupid? You think I don't know what you're doing? Narcissism isn't political, it's just narcissism. Just don't get the clap."

Early in the summer, Philip and Alice declared a truce. What this amounted to was quieter arguments, no mention of Alice's sleeping around, and a slowing in the decay of their relationship. This lull in the hostilities, like a cease fire designed to exchange prisoners and recover bodies, was Philip's doing. He wanted Alice back. That was all he wanted.

And what did Alice want? Oblivion? At times it seemed that way. Maybe she wanted to punish someone for loving her, but that seemed too complicated, too perverse. Or maybe she wanted an end to the war, but then, when she was honest with herself, Alice realized that she had stopped thinking about it; she couldn't visualize it, not even with the TV images, the edges of it had clouded, it was just a story, something made up and unreal—and so, gradually, she understood that what she was doing with her protests and infidelities was something else, but she hadn't any idea what. Philip had seen through her and so she had to make herself opaque. Maybe, she kept worrying, it *was* death.

Disdain expressed calmly is still disdain, was Philip's thought.

"Philosophy isn't about loving wisdom, it's about winning arguments," Alice told her husband. She looked lovely saying it. She was gaunt and pale—a bodhisattva or a romantic tubercular patient—Millie Theale, thought Philip. She'd cut her hair short and wore the same jeans every day. Pretty women might lose their attractiveness by disregarding their appearance, but Alice was beautiful, and nothing could change that. Here, Philip knew, was another of the world's deceits—the more you love someone, the less they are inclined to love you in return. Philip saw that his wife's great anger had evoked some deeper, unspecified feelings in Alice; she had become indifferent, outwardly engaged but inwardly passive. For her part, it occurred to Alice that Philip was myopic—he only related to ideas, never to people. He was good in company, amusing and witty, but he never felt anything for his students and colleagues, nor did he have any real friends. Ideas were alive for him, statements about the world, propositions in logic, the history of psychology, the controversies in the journals.

He analyzed her, maddeningly, as if she were a problem in language or psychology.

"Dear Alice," Philip would begin, "the world isn't subject to our will. You cannot reason suffering away, or make sense of it, or, God knows, end it. History isn't the working out of reason and there's no *Geist*, no dialectic fits the chaos. Your guilt and obsessions aren't healthy, not for us and not for you."

These sentences might have charmed Alice a year ago. Now she ground her teeth.

"And what of you Philip? Do you suppose moving words around has any worth? Do your articles help anyone? I mean, really Philip, who cares about John Stuart Mill? Who even knows who he was? At least my obsessions are up to date."

Philip hated when his wife attacked his work. He loved his profession and had convinced himself that it had transcendent importance. He began to dream of hurting her—not in any specific way, but every night, as he slept alone, he would lapse into a jumble of fractured images of Alice begging him to do something, or not to—he supposed in his dream state that she had become again the old Alice who had admired him. Had he been wrong about that? Yes, perhaps he had been vain from the beginning, misreading the signs. Egos were monstrous things. How easy it is to become a fool, Philip thought. And then he grew angry, angry at the slogans that everyone shouted around campus and spoke in his classes, and wrote in essays on Descartes or Hume. One student told him in a private conference that he was ashamed to be a student at a good college; he was thinking of quitting. Another offered that he planned to change his major to business—business!—because there was no point in the liberal arts anymore and he thought he'd like to make some money. How comforting it must be to give up seriousness for a cause, how gratifying to use the word 'struggle' or to talk about 'the people' or to go on about 'democracy', as if these kids whose idea of privation was cold pizza had any idea what real struggle entailed. Let them try to register black voters in D.C. as Philip once had, or spend a month living among the *favelados* in **Cidad de Deus**, in Rio, as he did, years before, back when Alice and her *comrades* were learning how to color inside the lines. Philip had come by his irony honestly. It had been earned—he had seen suffering, done a few things that he didn't brag about. But now he saw that he was a vain and foolish man. He'd married the wrong woman. She'd seduced him and he had helped her, and then she had been disappointed that he was exactly what he appeared to be—an outsider who loved books.

It was too complicated, even for a philosopher. When Philip got into these recursive loops of thinking about how he thought about his wife, he could only laugh at his folly, have a glass of Scotch, and shut himself up in his study.

"What are you working on?" Alice would sometimes ask, but Philip understood she had no interest.

"Nothing really. A rebuttal to Scott."

"Interesting."

Philip hated this word. Dog shit was interesting.

"Not at all. Dry and pedantic, academic hair-splitting. This is an argument about the value of life. Whether it's an absolute or a relative value, and what's entailed by how you think about this question. There are cases where suicide is the right course, abortion, execution, just war. Nobody knows how to decide these kinds of questions. Kant was wrong about our moral sensibility. There isn't one. And without that, without and normative laws, we grope toward some standards. That's what philosophers do. *Remember?*"

It was here that Alice and Philip lost each other.

A life, Alice understood, changed in an instant. Something disrupts what you assume, or a person you've come across reveals a part of herself, or a part of yourself, that makes everything else seem clear, or not clear, or just too different to be manageable under the rules you have long regarded as fixed. And so you change the rules according to which you live, or you don't, it doesn't matter, because nothing can be the same anymore. Her life changed just then: 'Remember?'

During the summer, just after Alice's run in with the DC police, at a time when his wife was vulnerable, Philip decided that they might save their marriage—that he might save his wife—by taking a trip together. Academics regard travel as inherently a good thing, as if being somewhere else automatically allows one to start over. Philip, given to gestures, called it The Reconciliation. Alice wasn't enthusiastic about reconciliation, but liked the idea of a trip south. They flew to Bridgetown in Barbados and took a room in a lovely and overpriced hotel. The island was a speck of white sand in the midst of an enormous blue globe of sea and sky. The ocean was flat and endless: one could walk from the porch of the Royal Hotel for a hundred yards and be standing in water that was the temperature of blood. Philip was pale and thin in his bathing attire (as he called it); Alice wore a black suit that turned the heads of the tourists who lounged around the pool. In his low-key way, Philip was jealous. Alice reveled in the heat and humidity, the dark, star-studded sky, the men who waited on her, admiring her long legs and flat belly. She felt as if it had been cold forever; the dark skies of Washington had oppressed her, but even the tropical sun could not thaw her heart.

She and Philip made love once or twice, but without feeling. Alice was detached, and she could feel the sadness in Philip's hands as he touched her.

"There isn't much point is there?" said Philip.

"I don't know what you mean."

Philip stroked Alice's hair. He touched her breasts and pushed his hand down her stomach, prying her legs apart.

"You do know about cruelty don't you? About how it works on others, what it does to the sadist?"

"Please Philip, no riddles now. Would you like to make love? I feel up to it and I can see you are as well."

"What an expression. 'To make love.' Is that what we do?"

Alice wanted more than anything to get up from the damp bed, to shower and dress, to walk alone on the beach. Her detachment surprised her, but there was nothing she could do about it.

Philip rolled away from Alice and picked up a book from the end table.

"Listen to this Alice, I think it applies to us. '*The woman opened a window, a tongue of sun came in. Everything was worn, there were too many things in the room. Boxes stacked up in the corners, piles of newspapers. The woman murmured an excuse and vanished into the dark mouth of a hallway. The Lieutenant heard a canary trilling somewhere. Was she really his wife?'* Yes, of course, she was his wife 'before God,' is what Llosa writes. Do you think Alice that there are too many things in our room, too many boxes and piles? Do you wish to vanish like the wife in the story, down some dark hallway, away from me?"

Alice began to cry.

"You know I dream of you every night, and the dream is always the same. You are leaving, going on a train or a bus, or you are walking away, not waving, walking quietly down a dark street, alone or sometimes with a man. At first I thought the man in the dream was me, and then I knew he wasn't, even though I couldn't see his face I knew he was a stranger. And you are always beautiful in the dream, just like now, long and slender, but hard as stone. And you never say anything to me, never a word. Isn't that a sad dream? For us to have been married for a few months, and for me to dream this sad dream."

They were quiet for a while. Philip holding his book but of course not reading; Alice crying, but without conviction. Each of them was thinking how much they wished they might be anywhere else, with anyone else, or, better, alone. As the silence lengthened the philosopher and his wife each realized how little they felt. Philip was stoical and committed to a certain course of living. He would survive whatever occurred, and though he would have preferred Alice's company to solitude, he was unable to think of a sentence he might utter that wouldn't be untrue, a betrayal of who he was. For her part, Alice felt disappointment in her husband—she had expected more from him, more understanding, greater empathy, a break with the past that would commit him entirely to her life. She had imagined a merging of their identities; instead they existed in some vague contiguous space filled only by the tedium of ordinary life. Nothing had been transformed or altered in Alice's heart. The politics had been important, and perhaps still were important, but now Alice understood that something else was missing. Of course, what was missing was love. What else could matter? She understood this. She didn't love Philip and never had. And most likely he had never loved her. If he had, if she had, this moment would not have occurred.

"Philip?"

"What?"

"Can we please have sex? I don't want to talk anymore. Please."

Later on they slept, and then dressed in silence. Some resolution had come to them, but neither Philip nor Alice understood what it entailed. They would wait.

<hr>

With her father in the hospital, Alice returned to Philadelphia to pack her things and arrange for a leave of absence from graduate school. She had no idea how long she would be gone, or what she and her father would live on apart from his Social Security. The thought of leaving her apartment and the life that she had so painstakingly built up out of the ashes of her past was distressing. On the other hand, nothing much was going to come of what she was doing now. Alice knew she wouldn't finish her degree, knew that the department was impatient with her slow pace and eccentric interests, knew that, at some point, she would have to decide what would come next—well, the decision had been made for her.

The days she had spent at home had enhanced her dreaminess. Driving to Philadelphia from the hospital, Alice reconstructed her marriage to Philip. She did this only to absolve herself of guilt—something that seemed both important and impossible. And then Cambodia came up, as it always did, a flashback, irrepressible and terrible. Writing about the genocide began as a means of controlling her memories. Philip had once told her that the consolation of philosophy wasn't in finding the truth, but in looking for it. That seemed right. No logic could comprehend atrocity, but the honorable task of preserving a record had insulated Alice from the past. She dreaded the loss of this work; the last thing she wished was for time to think.

There wasn't a lot to do. When she arrived back in Philadelphia, Alice wrote a note to her department chairman requesting an emergency leave of absence. She packed up her books and clothes but decided to abandon her furniture. She called the landlord to say she would be moving out and that of course she understood that he would keep her deposit. Sometime during that afternoon Alice sat down with a cup of tea to think about how quickly she was able to unbind herself from the life she had been living for the past five years. She had a few friends, Cambodians and Vietnamese men and women living in exile, though now the place they had left had faded from their minds.

We are all in exile, thought Alice, separated from some-place or from some person who was our home. Rootlessness is the norm. Nothing means more than stability achieved through habit.. You can't go back; you can't do things over again. Her parents never left the place where they grew up. What had been so charming about their world? One place can take the place of every other; we live in our own minds, or at least the richest part of our lives is there, inside. But then, Alice thought, leaving was what I wanted. Experience, how I yearned for it, how endless the possibilities seemed! Alice drank tea and then Scotch and went around the same tired thoughts.

The Scotch took the edge off of her anxiety, and after a while she could lie down and rest, she could dream about her mother and notice even as she dreamed that her mother's face was not quite as clear as it had been a few days before. The lights, Alice thought, were dimming, as if the play had ended and the audience—that is, Alice—was gathering her things to leave, collecting her thoughts so as to go back outside into the cold night alone.

—⁓—

In 1972, when Alice was in Cambodia and thinking about how she had come to be there, she clarified for herself, in a way that was satisfying but, she knew, quite false, the course of her actions. It is sometimes said that it is people who draw us away from our accustomed lives, who lure us into circumstances that seem, in retrospect, unthinkable. But at first Alice felt no connection to the people of Cambodia. The men and women she met, whose language she learned to speak reasonably well, whose foods she learned to eat, whose music—at first grating and childish—she came to enjoy, these men and women remained closed to her, not foreign in the way the landscape was foreign, but shut off from her in the way that the pages of a book written in Hebrew or Chinese were shut to her; she had no point of entry, no comprehension of what she was experiencing. It wasn't the people whom she came to love, or their struggle for survival, or their history, or the tragic fate inflicted on them by her own country and its mad rulers—it was none of these things that moved Alice, or that changed her life.

⁓⁓⁓

When the 'Great Reconciliation' was over—Philip used air quotes and implied capital letters—he and Alice returned to take up the life that they had been living. Philip was teaching undergraduate classes in logic and the history of philosophy, and one graduate course in the American pragmatists. He had a theory about Dewey, and he was thinking of writing a book about how Dewey and Santayana had pushed American thought in a new direction. What direction? Alice asked the question, but ignored the answer, which, in the manner of philosophy, was both uninteresting and overly complicated. Dewey, Philip explained, was the only American thinker to deny the existence of the self as a reflection of the world. There were, apparently, profound epistemological and metaphysical implications, though Alice wasn't sure she understood them. She asked Philip if he proposed to become a Buddhist, and he laughed at her and said no he wasn't talking about that kind of negation of the self but rather the one that goes back to Descartes, with its 'inner being' that dreams up 'clear and distinct' ideas for the person to believe in like *God* and *meaning* and *truth*. Platonism in other words, but dressed up in rationalist guise. *No self* might also mean that there are no inner meanings, maybe no meanings at all, maybe just a bunch of empty words and objects that take on significance as they are adapted to a person's life. Alice had an insight.

"That would be the end of philosophy, right, if there were no more meanings to argue about?"

"That's right," said Philip. "The end of all arguments. You always were the brightest student."

A month after their return to Washington, Alice thought about moving out, but she didn't want to give up on Philip, or marriage, or perhaps herself, but then there was the question of why she didn't wish to give up—around and around she went. Philip's mind was closed to her, as all minds are closed to those who don't inhabit them. Empathy aside, we are strangers to one another, as Philip was fond of reminding Alice. Alice *tried* to understand, to love, to change. In her mind, "tried" was always placed in quotation marks, but, she thought, he is too immersed in himself, in his work, in his collegial arguments with other self-absorbed cerebral men—"I have 'tried,' but to no avail." These little internal colloquies might go on as she sat silently at dinner, or in the midst of an informal gathering of his students. She would look at a man she admired and "try" to understand why her passion had cooled. Had she changed, or had he? Alice had little experience of other people's feelings—perhaps, she admitted to herself, none—but one thing she thought she knew was that change came suddenly, at least in what cuts deepest. She "tried" to work this out, at night, awake, alone often as her husband trundled off to read tedious Victorian novels—*Adam Bede* that month—in his study, more alone than she had ever been, for, she discovered, the loneliness that comes with being with someone whom you no longer feel affection for is far worse than any other—it more like losing a limb than anything she could imagine, "An imperial affliction/Sent us of the Air" was how her favorite poet put the matter, though Miss Dickinson might not have been speaking of love, no one knew, Alice believed that she was, for there could be no hurt so afflicting as this. Alice "tried" and failed to make sense of what had happened. After a while, she gave up and decided to leave her inner life alone and to focus instead on a career. She applied for a job in the State Department, using her brief experience in Cambodia, her rudimentary Khmer language skills, and her few contacts at Georgetown as an entrée. She hadn't much hope, but the life she had been living was over.

—⁓—

The day that she expected to return to her childhood home—a day that she would remember as the longest of her life—began inauspiciously. She had too much to drink the night before, fell asleep in her clothes, and drifted from one disquieting dream to another.

When she woke up, she was drenched in sweat. She drank a glass of water and took a shower. Finished packing her books. But she no longer felt any sense of urgency. She didn't make the phone calls that she had planned to make. When she had finished packing she stacked her things up by the front door of her apartment, but didn't take them to the car. She made eggs and coffee and sat for a long time in the dim sunlight that brushed through her window. She daydreamed and tried to cry but couldn't. She worked on her writing, but got nowhere. She looked at the pages of a book, but it was blank. Then she gave up and simply sat still. *Everyone has these kinds of days* is what she thought. These are the days that seem endless and that we remember forever. I have already had more than my share of these long, empty days—and there will be more of them. It occurred to her to turn on the radio, but she chose not to.

There was to be a new president sworn in today, though she hadn't followed the campaign or the election at all, having decided, years before, that there were two fundamental truths about American politics: first, there was no such thing; second, what was called 'politics' was simply a form of business in which the chief commodity was power. Since politics had destroyed her marriage and nearly taken her life, she thought it best to pay no attention.

She decided to go out, to the library. The Van Pelt was the one place she felt comfortable. It had been her refuge during the past five years, a place she went to read and write and think—to daydream. She would spend the day, her last in Philadelphia, in the comfort of the library. She tidied herself up a little, brushed her hair, and walked out into the cold morning. The sun was dim, arching toward an early exit—snow littered the sidewalks and was piled high at the curb. Cars were snowed in, covered with gritty black piles of frozen filth. It was a weekday, and busy, though the street people and unemployed among her neighbors were nowhere to be seen. She wasn't going to work, just to sit for a while, return a few books that she wouldn't be able to take with her, perhaps say goodbye to a couple of friends who, she knew, would be occupying their carrels, indifferent to the weather, the coronation, the world as it spun through winter and toward an uncertain, and distant spring.

⸻

In the autumn of 1970, Alice told Philip that she had been accepted for a position with the State Department. She told Philip that this had been her wish since her first trip to Cambodia. He said that it was odd that she hadn't mentioned this desire before, but he didn't press the point. Alice said that she was surprised to be hired, but elated. The government, on the strength of her language skills, and prior experience, was offering her an opportunity to take a posting, a temporary job, in Southeast Asia. In Phnom Penh. She would go? Yes, she wanted more than anything to do something like this, something important. She was tired of college. And, Philip wondered, did she want a divorce him before leaving. Not at all. Alice assured Philip that she only wanted some time apart, a chance to "do something in the real world." She still had to return to finish her degree; this would be temporary, six months, a year at most. She would return. Perhaps things would be better then. Philip was no fool. He knew that separations are never temporary; no wounds are healed by being ignored. But he was hardly in a position to keep Alice from doing as she wished. It was the Seventies. Slavery had been abolished. The Civil Rights Act had been passed. No one expected women to sit around waiting on their husbands. Everyone had rights. Philip repeated this hollow catechism to himself as he held his wife's hand.

166

They were walking along the Potomac on a breezy October day—the best season in Washington, the one that elated Philip each year as it dulled memories of the interminable summer. The Potomac looked clear as it sweep past the hotels and offices of Arlington. Alice told him about her hopes and plans, her excitement over the prospect of 'real' employment. Wasn't it odd to want to work for the government, given her feelings of just a few months ago? Working for the war machine? Alice had an answered prepared that wasn't convincing. Working in diplomacy was a way of ending wars, of heightening awareness about countries so that war could be avoided. Philip was prepared to rebut this absurd reasoning, but kept quiet. She mentioned again how important it was to 'do something real' in the world. Philip thought that his wife used this formula too often, as if living with him, going to school—however intermittingly—and attempting, however futilely, to build their marriage, were "doing nothing." Couldn't she see how degrading this kind of talk was, couldn't she understand that she was being selfish? No, it was his fault. It was his absurd pursuits, his pointless arguments, his commitment to a tradition that was dead and gone—what use was he in a world gone mad? Alice was right. She should do more with herself. She was young, vivacious. And he would move on too. He had no wish, and, worse, no ability to keep Alice at home. So, he blessed her, wished her *bon voyage*, and said, not really meaning it, that he looked forward to a time when they might be together again. Alice smiled in a way that killed the last of Philip's hope.

The empty smile of goodbye.

⁓

III.

Notes on the Death of Cambodia
by Alice Nye Turley

A country is its history, languages, faiths, and livelihoods. People tied to land and traditions. What does it take to eradicate a nation, to wipe it from the map? Pay attention.

The first sign of what was to come was the increased plotting by Lon Nol against Prince Sihanouk. Rumors of a coup against the government had circulated through Phnom Penh for years, but that the Prince's rule had become too precarious to continue now dominated thinking in the Western embassies and among the CIA operatives who moved back and forth between the capital and, covertly, the eastern sectors of the country—the jungle bordering South Vietnam where Sihanouk permitted North Vietnamese supply bases to remain, despite his concern that such actions would plunge his country into a wider regional war. At the American Embassy, I was placed on a team of analysts assigned to draft a contingency plan of US action in the event of a successful coup. The Ambassador confided to us his view that Sihanouk would devise a scheme to survive. The Prince was a wily politician, brutal and charming, and had succeeded in outliving his opponents for decades. He represented Cambodia to the world, traveled among Western capitals seeking peace and aid, and he moved with equal facility between Hanoi and Beijing. So astute a politician could not be removed by Lon Nol, a former police chief and security officer—hardly a figure with the stature of Sihanouk.

One must recall that it was Sihanouk himself who brought Lon Nol into the government, in 1966. The Prince regarded Lon Nol as a non-entity, as someone who lacked military abilities and appeared to have no strong political views. Besides, Lon Nol was thought to admire the Prince. Perhaps he did. Because Lon Nol seldom spoke, Sihanouk thought him dull, a man of few talents and no ambitions. I was told, "Lon Nol was 'silent as a carp,' and thought little of by all of us. We were wrong to underestimate him." I thought about silence and what it might mean as the country was falling apart. We know the CPK was already prepared to seize power, but had little strategic idea of how to do so. Their leaders were following the orders of the Vietnamese. By 1967, the Samlaut uprising had begun in northwestern Cambodia. Sihanouk began a three-year battle against the country's leftists, and the population, tired of the government's corruption, turned away from him.

The most dangerous enemy is always a friend.

In 1967, Sihanouk began to attack the leftist opposition with greater fervor. The "three ghosts"—Hou Youn, Hu Nim, and Khieu Samphan—and many young people joined the CPK in the forest. The anti-government, anti-Sihanouk movement was fueled by anti-American sentiment, a lack of economic opportunity, and by ethnic divisions within the country. A resumption of relations with the United States fueled the opposition; many Cambodians admired the Maoist revolution in China and wished their nation to follow the lead of China into a brighter, socialist future. At the Embassy, there was uncertainty as to how to proceed; members of the mission put out feelers to former government officials, including Sirik Matak, deputy prime minister and an inveterate opponent of Sihanouk. In a sense, Sihanouk—creator of modern Cambodia—was no longer relevant. Meanwhile, Vietnamese communists were occupying portions of eastern Cambodia.

When the coup finally came, in March 1970, Sihanouk was out of the country. Lon Nol engineered a no-confidence vote in the Prince's government, and, with the support of the United States—for this had been the recommendation of the embassy report—the Khmer Republic was declared. The *Gouvernement Royal d'Union Nationale du Kampuchéa*, including the Khmer Rouge, survived for exactly five years before being overthrown by Saloth Sâr—Pol Pot—and his followers.

President Nixon and Henry Kissinger favored the widening of the war as a means of diffusing American responsibility and providing, as it were, a smokescreen for the repatriation of U.S. combat troops. By 1970, anti-Vietnamese sentiment was so intense that massacres of Vietnamese civilians were carried out in the capital. Lon Nol was unable or unwilling to control the soldiers who gunned down innocent people. Prince Sihanouk, from Beijing, issued calls for "revolt" against the government of Lon Nol and for armed resistance against the Vietnamese occupying Cambodia. The CPK declared the Prince to be the "chairman" of their movement.

We investigated the policies and history of the Khmer Rouge, as well as those of other anti-Sihanouk factions within the country. The task force of which I was a part traveled outside of Phnom Penh to develop a more accurate feeling for the mood of the people. The "people" were frightened. No one understood at this early date (1971-1972) what the Khmer Rouge stood for, or what their burgeoning movement represented. It appeared to many peasants that the political situation would not effect them. Intellectuals—government cadres, officers, petit-bourgeois shopkeepers and the larger landowners—anticipated a widening of the war in neighboring Vietnam, but not to such an extent that it would impinge on their lives. These groups supported the Prince and wished above all for their neutrality to be respected by combatants in a war they viewed with increasing trepidation. During these early years of my posting in Cambodia there was much to do and a daunting amount to learn. We were often so busy that we didn't have time to process the information that we had gathered—much of this work was done by CIA analysts assigned to the Embassy or posted in Saigon. The world around me seemed thick with mystery, full of people with whom I couldn't communicate, an alien world of new smells and sounds and tastes that made me feel as if I had left the earth altogether. I tried not to think about how I was being affected by what was going on around me, but rather immersed myself in the rapidly changing, and as it happened, degenerating situation. In this effort I was only partially successful.

After the coup, with the Prince out of the country, there was a brief period of calm. Everyone held his breath, waiting for Lon Nol to act, waiting to see if the delicate coalition he had created would hold. Waiting, above all else, for the Khmer Rouge to define its role in the government. We had no clear policy directives to offer Washington, but then Washington wasn't interested in recommendations. Cambodian policy was being made in Saigon.

"I am going to return home to fight," was what Prince Sihanouk told Zhou Enlai when he arrived, in exile, in Beijing. The North Vietnamese made overtures to Pol Pot, hoping to create an alliance that would benefit them in their struggle against the United States. Sihanouk, proud and out of touch with reality, allowed himself to be lured into a position of dependence on the Khmer Rouge. He proclaimed the establishment of the National United Front of Kampuchea to fight Lon Nol—with an army created by the Chinese. I spent much of this time in my office in the American Embassy reading cables, writing or editing position papers for the Ambassador, summarizing daily events and some intelligence reports that crossed my desk, and preparing press briefings for reporters in Phnom Penh. All of us, I suppose, were unaware of the plotting that took place the spring of 1971. It was my view that Lon Nol's commitment to the West meant a better life for the mass of the Cambodian people. How little I understood....

The Chinese played the Prince, played the Cambodia card with cynicism and cunning. The 'Appeal of March 23,' likened to a kind of declaration of independence for the peoples of Southeast Asia, was in fact the work of Zhou Enlai and Pol Pot. Though Zhou was willing to use Sihanouk's international standing to build a case against Lon Nol's government, Pol Pot had no intention of becoming part of a coalition government. The country would belong to the Khmer Rouge.

Saloth Sâr, Pol Pot, First Brother, Grand Uncle. A diminutive man. Outwardly friendly, warm. Inside, who could tell? A one-time school teacher, just another face in the crowd. Pol Pot loved music and books, flirted with Buddhism, had girlfriends and chums while in school. Enjoyed cooking and practical jokes. Like other Cambodians, like Sihanouk himself, Sâr did not believe that Vietnam was an independent country—it was, had been, would be, a part of Kampuchea. Saigon was *Prey Nokor* in Khmer. Sâr visited that city in 1949 as a student. He was pleased to hear Khmer spoken, along with French and of course Vietnamese. Sâr smiled often on that trip; he was an engaging man. A journalist wrote that the Khmer smile was "like a screen hiding an emptiness that has been deliberately created as an ultimate defence against any who might wish to penetrate the secret of one's innermost thoughts." Sâr made friends readily. He kept his politics to himself, not speaking of his views except to his closest associates. His was an emptiness that would be filled by ambition.

I arrived in Phnom Penh in February 1971.

"But let me tell you on this business on Cambodia—I want something done tonight. I don't want any screwing around and I want the Air Force to make its study immediately of anything in conventional World War II type of craft that can be used over there. I want a new plan. I want it fast and let's get going." December 9, 1970, Nixon to Kissinger.

In November 1971 I wrote to Philip and told him that the situation in Cambodia was deteriorating and that I was needed in Phnom Penh. He did not reply for a month, and by the time I received his reply—an impassioned plea for me to come home—the situation in the country had deteriorated further. I did not answer his letter. We had no further correspondence until I returned to the United States.

Sâr was at a base camp code-named K-1, in the northern part of the country, near Dângkda. Pol Pot was fully dedicated to building an effective Khmer-Maoist army; half of the country was under communist control, and he was determined not only to extend the occupation of territory but also, by cooperating with forces of the North Vietnamese Army and Viet Cong, forces that were using Cambodia to launch a final series of devastating attacks against South Vietnam, to solidify the hold of the Khmer Rouge over the Cambodian people. Pol Pot managed to hold ground that the Khmer Rouge forces had gained, and by 1971 was proceeding to win—through propaganda and terror—the support of the Cambodian people, mainly the peasantry. Pol Pot and Nuon Chea, Ping Say and Hu Nim—key Khmer Rouge leaders—were convinced that only a totalitarian regime, one based on coercion and force, could bring the majority of the Cambodian people to support a government that would foster the collective good of the nation as a whole. The Khmer Rouge was determined from the outset of the Revolution to destroy their enemies and to exercise a reign of unselective terror throughout Cambodia, in the name of the 'collective happiness' of the Khmer people. To call this murderous fantasy 'communism' is to imply that there existed some historical rationale for what took place. There existed no such rationale. Killing for its own sake became the dystopian goal of the Khmer Rouge Revolution. *Years later as I wrote these words, I watched a film unfold, a film that consisted entirely of the faces of the dead.*

By the first anniversary of Lon Nol's coup, most Americans in Phnom Penh noted that fear had replaced optimism in the capital. Corruption was the rule, with American funds that were intended to support the Lon Nol

government being channeled into the pockets of government officials. My bosses at the Embassy, several of whom
were CIA agents, feared that Lon Nol's government would
fall, but officials in Washington had no interest in bad news,
or any interest in the complexity of Cambodian politics.
They were focused on Vietnam, and the troubles of the
Khmer Republic were a sideshow. Those in the Embassy
were told not to state their views on the ongoing crisis, or
to imply that leaders other than the incompetent Lon Nol
were better suited to guide the government through a war
with the Communist Party of Kampuchea. By the end of
1972, Lon Nol had eliminated all traces of democratic rule
and, in a fixed election, had himself declared president,
prime minister, defense minister, and head of the armed
forces. There was talk of evacuating the Embassy, but I had
no desire to leave. None of us did. We worked twenty-hour
days, overseeing programs set up by NGOs and monitor-
ing the intelligence that flowed into the Embassy from a
dozen agencies. Over two hundred million dollars in direct
aid was being channeled into the country to support the
Lon Nol government, to maintain the armed forces, to
pay security forces, and strengthen the hand of American
troops operating on the border with South Vietnam. In
March 1973, a disgruntled Cambodian Air Force officer
commandeered a T-28 bomber and released two bombs
that were intended for the presidential palace. The bombs
missed their target and incinerated two of the housing
complexes built for state workers. Fifty people were killed,
many of them children. Lon Nol declared a state of siege
and began to arrest his enemies. Despite the repression,

the government was only months away from falling. The Khmer Rouge had begun its final assault on Phnom Penh.

In the summer of 1973, my immediate supervisor at the Embassy, a CIA agent working as a communications expert, sent me into the field. I was assigned a jeep and a driver and for several weeks I traveled in widening circles around the capital. My assignment was to ascertain the level of support for the government.

"There is little support for the government," I told the agent.

"We don't know that for sure. I'm sending three teams out to gather intelligence."

"People here in the capital are frightened. Half of them support the CPK. The bombers are doing their work for them, that and the government."

"You're wrong. Washington thinks the situation can be stabilized. The bombings are against clean military targets."

"That's not what I hear."

"Consider this a friendly request. Take Sen Treng and visit some of the villages south and east of here. Don't go more than fifty kilometers. Talk to some people. Listen to what's being said. In one week I want a written report. I'll collate the intel and cable it to Saigon. We're operating blindly. Just because the troops are pulling out doesn't mean it's over. We're staying here to run this show for as long as possible."

"Sure. But let's not prejudge this thing. If you don't like what I find don't bury it."

"That's not going to happen."

In the last year a story had been concocted by some of the security and intelligence personnel at the Embassy. An article of faith was that the Cambodian people were anti-communists and would never support the CPK. That the Khmer Rouge was disorganized and ineffectual. That the bombings had been "sterile." I had been in the country for three years by this time, spoke Khmer fluently, and had plenty of contacts among the population—in all sectors. I was hearing a different story. The B-52 raids were pushing thousands of young peasants into the Khmer Rouge. The cadres were well organized, armed with Chinese rifles, and committed to overthrowing the Lon Nol government. The administration in Washington had been uninterested in Cambodia for too long, and their attempts to catch up with the situation were futile.

I stayed too long.

Massive B-52 raids were conducted in Cambodia, by order of President Nixon. Perhaps sixteen thousand CPK fighters were killed. Prince Sihanouk, his wife, and Ieng Sary secretly left China in order to tour the "liberated zones" under CPK control. The Prince and his wife, Monique, were comfortable on their journey, staying in "little chalets," as the Princess put it later in a published account of the trip. Sihanouk met with all of the major Khmer Rouge leaders, including Pol Pot. Upon his return to China he pronounced himself to be fully behind the Communist revolution in his country. The CPK controlled perhaps seventy percent of Cambodia, and was steadily tightening its grip on Phnom Penh.

—⁓—

On a steaming day in July 1973, my driver and I approached the provincial capital of Kompong Chhnang. Just outside the city, Sen Treng and I came upon a small group of CPK cadres, armed with AK-47s and M-16s. The soldiers were mostly boys, but clearly hardened by combat. The leader of the squad, an older man who had a wispy mustache, a shrunken chest, and who wore the checkered *krama* of the Party, waved the jeep to a halt. Sen Treng pulled over and spoke to the group's leader. The soldiers did not point their guns at the jeep, but they were alert.

"Where are you going?"

"To Kompong Chhnang."

"The city is closed."

"Why is it closed?" I asked.

"No questions."

"Was it bombed?"

"Many are dead and wounded."

"Perhaps we can help?"

"You are not needed." Pointing to me: "You're French?"

"American. From the Embassy."

"Get out of the jeep."

We did as we were told. Two of the cadres went to the jeep and removed my kit bag. The leader of the squad took it and opened it, spilling the contents on the ground. The young man stuffed the papers back into the kit bag and tossed it to one of his men. He pointed his own weapon at Sen Treng and said "Leave now."

182

"What about her?"

"She stays."

"You can't hold her. She is an American citizen."

The leader of the group pointed his weapon at Sen Treng. He looked at me and got into the jeep.

—⁓—

I was taken to a Khmer Rouge base camp in the jungle. I was released a week later. Aside from dehydration, I was physically intact. I was taken to Po Chentong airport by two men dressed in civilian clothes. Later, I returned to the Embassy.

—⁓—

Two agents debriefed me. I told them what I remembered, but there were lapses in my recollection. Because they insisted on many details that I was unable to supply, I made many things up to satisfy them. When the agents insisted that I repeat certain details, I was unable to do so, having been throughout my life an artless liar. One of the two—a man I had never seen at the Embassy before—grew angry with me and insinuated that I was deliberately hiding information that could be of vital importance. I said—"Vital in what way?" And he replied that our government was attempting to formulate a policy of 'flexible response'— his exact words—to the unfolding situation in Cambodia. I might have smiled at this, or shaken my head as he grew heated and more impatient with my account of the time I spent in the jungle. I quoted a line from Clausewitz that I had heard Philip repeat on a couple of occasions as an argument against the Vietnam War: "War is an act of force and there is no logical limit to the application of that force." The agent demanded to know what I meant by this statement—apparently he hadn't read Clausewitz—and I replied only that 'flexibility' had no meaning anymore. We were in a place where limits did not apply, and so I didn't think my views would have any bearing on the outcome. This answer didn't satisfy him, but I had nothing more to say. I wanted to tell the truth, but I knew it didn't matter—what I had seen convinced me that Cambodia was doomed, that our 'mission' here was over, that it would only be a short time before we would be compelled to leave. I didn't say this to the agents, to the Ambassador—he was kind to me, and asked only how I felt—or to other members of the Embassy staff. Sen Treng was solicitous, and apologetic, but what could he have done? He would have been shot. The people who took me were capable of anything—to have shot Sen Treng would have been like swatting a mosquito. I told him: "You are alive because you did what they told you to do. And I am alive for the same reason." He was grateful. In my heart I suppose I did blame him a little, but that was wrong of me. I rested for a few days and then went back to work. No one mentioned my captivity again. I tried not to think about what had happened, what I had seen. I tried to focus on my work, but was not able to do so. The situation became dire almost at once, and then, quickly, it was over.

<center>~~~</center>

The bombardments began earlier each day. After a while they didn't cease. We began to shred documents. The streets would be full of people for a few hours each morning, and then deserted. The gates of the Embassy were mobbed around the clock—Cambodians seeking exit visas. The airport was open, but irregularly; mortar rounds hadn't reached the runways yet, but there had been sappers and suicide bombers—two Cambodian air force jets had been destroyed. Helicopters stood ready, the Ambassador told us that we would be extracted from the compound. Time had run out. CIA agents disappeared during the night. Suddenly it seemed I was one of only a dozen members of the Embassy staff left. There was quiet panic in the Embassy—dread, and certain knowledge that the end had come.

The final days of Cambodia—the bombs now fell close to the Embassy—mortar rounds, the Marines said. A few American reporters were still in Phnom Penh and now they came to the Embassy hoping for transport to Bangkok. Low level personnel were taken to the airport in APCs and flown to Saigon where they would either be sent home or reassigned. I was asked if I wanted to leave and said that I did not.

Time sped up the last few days. Here are some images, from my diary, of what transpired during the last month. They are unedited. I admit to being unclear about some things.

—"They say the White Crocodile has returned. I heard women speaking of it in the market today, and, later, an old man mentioned him in my hearing at the Royal. A sign that the destiny of Cambodia is to change, that the river of time, the river of Cambodia's history, will now run in another direction."

—"Many reports are reaching the Embassy of bombs falling on rural villages. Targeting, said one of my colleagues, appears 'inept.'"

—"The Administration's problems are spilling over into the Embassy. There is concern about who is now making policy and what direction our 'work' here will take. At today's briefing, Bill Sizemore said that a protocol for evacuating Embassy personnel had been approved at State, and that 'in the event' of a further deterioration of the military situation, we would have sufficient advance warning of our evacuation. However, 'be prepared for a more expeditious departure.' Bill, who is the soul of confidence, seemed shaken by the rapidity of the CPK's advance toward the capital. I believe he knows as well as anyone that the army cannot defend the city and that it is now a matter of weeks, if not days, before the enemy arrives. I wanted to ask what would happen *when* the city fell, but I thought better of doing so."

—"It appears that the Khmer Rouge fighters are very brave, or perhaps, very much in love with dying. They charge fixed positions en masse, with no regard for casualties. One of the agents assigned to communications told me that he had been in on the interrogation of a young communist cadre and was told that his comrades 'have no fear of death, only of their officers.' It seems that any display of cowardice is punished by a bullet to the head— no questions asked. On the other hand, the agent told me the army of the Republic is full of unwilling soldiers, many of whom are deserting to the enemy out of fear, or out of hatred of Lon Nol's government. They feel betrayed on all sides. I supposed we too are a part of that betrayal."

—"It turns out that the puppet masters are the Chinese. While they parley with Nixon and Kissinger, the leadership in Beijing runs Sihanouk, putting him in touch with the Khmer Rouge, and, at the same time, uses Lon Nol. America is the enemy, and China uses the Khmer Rouge against them. They also use the Vietnamese. Lon Nol is hopeless, and in his insistence on making war in the north against the Vietnamese, he overstepped the limits of Chinese patience."

—"Lon Nol lives in the past. And soldiers of the Khmer Rouge, visionaries in their own way, die for the future. What could be more futile? Both Lon Nol and Saloth Sâr want what they can't have, each one is willing to kill innocent people to make their mad dreams come true. It has ever been so."

—The world is unreal, a tissue of illusion. Death and life are the same, or at least one needn't take account of any difference between the two. There is no 'self,' and certainly no soul. Why then should one not be in love with death? I can't accept this strain of Buddhist thought, and yet I respect those who do. How can Marxism be married to such otherworldliness? What could class struggle possibly mean to Sâr and the others who even now are massacring peasants twenty kilometers from here? Khmer Rouge isn't a political movement, it's a cult. Sâr is more like Jim

Jones than he is like Lenin. Perhaps I'm missing something. Perhaps this is what Marxism was about all along—millenarianism married to materialism, the destruction of this world so that the judgment of history can be finalized, so that punishment can be meted out.

—⁓—

Lists of our Cambodian friends were made by the CIA agents and the Ambassador. I understood that those on the lists would be evacuated and that those who were not on the lists might be killed because of their affiliation with the enemy. Everyone knew who worked for us—there were no secrets in the capital.

The Khmer Rouge was using the Mekong River to ferry men and supplies southward. Saigon was also under siege and the cessation of American air support for the South Vietnamese government signaled the end there as well. Planes full of approved persons left the airfield every few hours; C-130s packed with frightened allies of the Lon Nol government, each man clutching the allotted single suitcase, each mother holding her children. Pochentong Airport was no longer secure. Eighty-one millimeter mortar rounds fell throughout the day, at random intervals. The runways were pocked with craters. Fixed wing aircraft could no longer land. The Ambassador was driven in his bulletproof limo to the edge of strip and put aboard a helicopter with his family and close aides. He carried the American flag with him.

A drunken Marine told me that he wouldn't leave the Embassy, that he would "go down with the ship." I packed my things.

A group of Marines burned papers, including over two million dollars in Embassy funds.

The next morning, with the capital aflame, with artillery battering the outskirts of the city, I boarded a helicopter and was flown to Saigon. After a few days of debriefing, I was flown home. I had asked to stay, but those in authority told me that there was no longer anyplace I could stay. "We're through here," a MAC-V colonel told me. He was right, and I went home.

IV.

January 20, 1981

I am cold now. My feet are numb. I drink my coffee and wish that I had another. Seng made me dumplings with garlic sauce. He wouldn't take my money. His wife is angry with him for giving away food, but he tells her they are already rich and can afford it. Seng winks at me and rolls his eyes. His wife waves her arms and scolds him in Khmer. She also speaks French and Vietnamese. She won't speak Vietnamese around me, except to say good day or how cold it is—my face and wounded leg make her uncomfortable, my slow way of moving and speaking, and I know she wishes I would patronize one of the Chinese trucks across the street. Seng tells me in English to ignore her taunts—

"She is calling you a name."

"What? What is she calling me?"

"It is a word that means someone who takes for nothing."

"Freeloader."

"That's it. But more expressive."

"Then why won't you take my money."

"I can't. If I do, I am disgraced."

"Not with me you aren't. I owe you two fifty."

"Not important. Next time, maybe."

"I'll go Chinese for a while. Cool her down."

"No. That truck is bad. You will get diarrhea. Here, take another dumpling."

More angry words, but the dumplings are the best I've ever had. I wave to Seng and tell him to be careful. I say in Vietnamese, *please be happy today.*

The streets aren't deserted, but they are unpeopled by Philadelphia standards. It is cold and raw and there's a spectacle on television.

It feels like the heat is off. The basement is damp. The books are rotting, but no one seems to mind. Decay is all around us, seeping into the nooks of our lives in this city and nation—no, that's wrong. I do that, I generalize from my own experience, from the small piece of things that I see every day. Just say, it's damp, and I can smell the rot in the paper. Then again.

Up now, up, to the second floor, to science, to mathematics, the Qs and Rs and Ts for technology. Mornings are theoretical and humanistic—why not? Refreshed by a slow walk I can take care of the mechanical arts, the work of the hands, what the Greeks thought was beneath the man of virtue, Plato saying that no ruler could imitate a craftsman, no craftsman could lie, though rulers could and did. Here are books with no words, symbols run like hieroglyphics across the pages—Advanced Quantum Mechanics, Differential Equations for Engineers, Modal

Logic, Riemann's Paradox, Fermat's Paradox, Gödel's Paradox—the beauty of the Qs and Rs is here, recognition of paradox, of the fact that reason reaches an endpoint beyond which nothing more can be explained or known. Numbers might be embedded in the world in the way that Plato and Augustine thought, or they might be discovered there by geniuses like Newton and Euler and Cantor, though I suppose Newton believed that God had put the numbers there as esoteric clues to His Divine Plan.

The range in which carbon atoms can be constructed out of three helium atoms is ever so small—the bonding energy is something like seven million electron volts—less than that you get no carbon, more, same thing. That's the idea, though Newton wouldn't have known the details—little footprints of the Artist stowed away in the minute corners of His work. The trouble is, the footprints turn out to be evidence of nothing more than complexity, and complexity, as we know, can occur naturally—that's pretty much the way of things. Reading here in these stacks over the past few years has convinced me that the universe is the deadliest and most inhospitable place imaginable. The only reason it seems miraculous that I'm sitting on the floor among the Rs in the Van Pelt Library in Philadelphia on this January afternoon is that I am. We're here among the accidents.

In this handbook—why do they call it a *handbook* as no hand could comfortably accommodate its 1200 pages?—the physics of firearms. $C=SD/I=w/i$ Where C is the ballistic coefficient, SD is the sectional differential, and i is the drag coefficient. I should not be thinking about this, but something this morning forced the memory to come to life and now it is irresistible. For example, the bullet that penetrated my leg and hip, as well as the bullet that killed the kid from Claxton, had a ballistic coefficient of .272. This number refers to the ease with which a projectile is able to pass through the air—how well does a point of steel and copper pierce the air of Mu Duc on an April day? How many grams of gunpowder—potassium nitrite, sulphur, and charcoal—does it take to launch this projectile with a velocity sufficient to break apart the acetabulum of my hip joint?

There is a precision in things, in the world. Let's imagine that we could measure every event in the way this one episode can be measured. Perhaps there is a formula hidden in some cranny of God's universe into which the past and present could be weighed like the thirty grams of gunpowder that propelled a bullet with the ballistic coefficient of .272. In the library of the infinite this information exists. The beauty of this fancy. Imagine the numbers, written in the Egyptian manner, no place holders, little images of tadpoles and fish and gesticulating stick figures standing for five or ten thousand of something, and they are—imagine it—embedded in the stars from which we have come. Embedded then in some unimaginable way in us. God made all things in number, weight, and measure.

"Notwithstanding all differences between the physical problems which have given rise to the development of relativity theory and quantum theory, respectively, a comparison of purely logical aspects of relativistic and complementary argumentation reveals striking similarities as regards the renunciation of the absolute significance of conventional physical attributes of objects." Niels Bohr, writing in the Einstein *Festschrift*: I am sitting among dozens of German and Danish titles focused on the problems of modern physics. The books have yellow paper; the spines crack and emit the dusk of glue and the north woods. No one ever comes to this range—science moves forward too quickly for archives to have utility. I bury my nose in the *Zeitschrift für Physik*, the volume from 1927. The aroma is of Weimar and high modernism, the end of classical physics and of the hopeful Enlightenment. It reminds me of *Magic Mountain* and *Young Törless*. I can read many of the words, but they ringed about with mathematical symbols that mean nothing. The pages are beautiful, like Gorky's or de Kooning's paintings of the 40s, etched morphic shapes that speak to us in an unknown language.

Classical physics was an idealization. In dealing with the relatively large, observable masses of everyday experience, Newtonian mechanics worked well. With Boltzmann's model of the atom, and, in particular, with Planck's discovery of the constant of quantum action, the notion that the classical model could hold for the subatomic realm had to be abandoned—as did the idea of causality itself, the bedrock of a rational system of the world. The "renunciation of the conventional" is understatement: what Bohr did was overturn reason in the way that David Hume first imagined one could do—and Einstein carried the lesson of the photoelectric effect to the precipice of quantum theory, a precipice that Bohr was quite willing to stare into—an abyss. Light is wave and particle, depending on how it is measured. When it is measured, the world is changed. The world is frozen light, and the uncertainty of matter, the unreliability of causality stretches from the black event horizons of dead stars to the incandescence that barely illuminates this corner of the Van Pelt. Heisenberg's word was *Ungenauigkeit*: the world at its subatomic core is *inexact*. If we are to be saved, we must have hope first of all, because the world is without mercy and the gods are without compassion.

The sun is waning. We have a new president.

Science can be comforting, but also disturbing. So many things are explicable using the theories of natural selection or Newtonian mechanics, but so much remains unproven. If my consciousness exists at the level of my neurons, if that is where "I" am to be found, then what about the effects of quantum mechanics on the atoms that make up my neurons? How sure can I be that I'm not a zombie, or that my brain isn't some sort of mechanism that has fooled me into thinking I am me? Who is it that is talking to me now, and how can this voice be connected to my brain? The problem of consciousness, of conscience, of free will. How can a purely material brain, with all of its attendant hormones and nerve endings choose to do anything? Jane has a new computer on her desk. She hates it. If she types the call letter QA756.879 instead of QA756.878 the computer will direct her to the wrong book, but if she goes to the shelf her eye will catch the error at once—she wanted Morris Klein's *Mathematics the Loss of Certainty* and there it is, misshelved by a work-study student. Descartes set up a little theatre of consciousness in us, and our souls are supposed by him to do all the business of thinking and feeling while the body tags along, somehow, detached from the whole affair. What would a soul be like? Ethery, like the wind that blows through my room at night, like the light bouncing off this range of ideas that flowed out of someone else's souls—it's magic, lovely to think about, difficult.

⸻

I am not a positivist. The absolute distinction between facts and values is not something I can accept; nor will I acknowledge that science alone can show us the best way to live. When I gave up on God I assumed that there would be no more grounds for holding any particular set of values. But my years reading here in the Van Pelt have convinced me otherwise. The numbers in the handbooks, the long lines of equations that purport to describe the world—that *do* describe its physical being—have their counterpart in the works of philosophy, literature, anthropology, history, and art that I read in the mornings. My notebooks are full of clues, chains of arguments that provide a clear rationale for believing that there is a correct way to live and that it can be discovered through a combination of thinking and feeling. Values come from third parties—no one is ever disinterested, but there are degrees of detachment that make it more likely one will behave properly. I have become a pragmatist. Hegel may have been right to see deeper forces at work in history; but they weren't spiritual forces, nor were they purely material. What do you get when you add spirit to matter?

—◦—

"What?"

"What are you doing here?"

"What do you mean?"

"You're sitting on the floor mumbling. Are you all right?"

"Yes, of course. I'm just thinking. Did I disturb you?"

"Of course you disturbed me. You were talking out loud. Why are you on the floor?"

"Because these are the books I need to look at—right here, on the bottom of the range. I can't bend over."

"I can see that. Could you try to be quieter then? I'm working right behind you."

"I know you."

"I don't think so."

"No, I mean I've seen you before. You're a graduate student."

"I am. But so is everybody else in here. I remember you from earlier. You were up in the Oriental Languages. I had the impression that you were spying on me."

"I was, sort of. You were speaking Khmer. I was trying to see if I could pick up anything. Just out of curiosity."

"That's rude."

"I know. I'm that way sometimes. Overbearing. I talk to myself, smoke on the landings, spill coffee in the carrels. But the librarians like me."

"You're not a student are you?"

"I'm a freelancer."

"You know Khmer?"

"A little. I apologize. You don't have to worry about me,

200

I'm harmless. The talking aloud just started a few months ago. It helps me to clarify what I'm thinking about. I have moments of unclarity. But I'm harmless."

"You were in Vietnam?"

"Yes. And Cambodia. Unofficially. That's where I heard Khmer."

"You speak Vietnamese?"

"Some."

"Korean?"

"Not a word."

"I speak Khmer. I lived there. I lived and worked there."

"That makes sense. Hard to learn Khmer any other way. You with the Red Cross, some NGO?"

"No. The government."

"Not the CIA. They say women make the best agents, but you don't look the type."

"There were plenty of agents in Phnom Penh, I worked with some. Good people and bad, like anyplace else. No, I was in the Embassy, right until the end."

"Can you do me a favor?"

"What?"

"Help me up. My goddamned leg."

"Jesus. You okay?"

"Give me a second."

"I'm sorry about before. I was rude. I didn't realize."

"Forget it. Guys like me freak people out."

"Not me. I'm sorry."

"Are there elephants in Cambodia?"

"I beg your pardon?"

"Are there elephants in Cambodia?"

"Yes. Some. Small ones, like in India. They're endangered, but there are some. I never saw one, but that's what I heard."

"Huh."

"So you really were there, in Cambodia?"

"Yes. But not to talk about."

"You were shot there?"

"More or less. Really, it's a sad story, not very uplifting. But a buddy of mine made some assertions about elephants and I've been meaning to check on that. So, listen, you want to sit down for a minute? I need to get off my feet."

"I have stuff to do. I don't have much time."

"It can wait. Come on. Do you smoke?"

"No. Smoking is disgusting."

"It is that. But we don't have to. Come on. Let's sit on the stairs. Five minutes of your time."

"Why? What do we have to talk about?"

"Probably nothing. But let's just see, just for a moment, if we can help each other."

"Help how?"

I looked at her, I don't know, seriously, or pleadingly. I looked the way you sometimes do when there's urgency, when time is short.

"Okay."

"What's your name?"

"Alice."

We went into the stairwell. I sat on the steps and Alice stood in front of me. After a while she sat down as well. She was a small woman, very pretty, dark, with eyes you don't forget—green, black lashes, weary but alert, the eyes of someone who paid attention. No makeup. Small, straight nose, good teeth. Tiny pearl earrings, maybe antiques, hair in a tight bun with a kind of comb pushed up inside to hold it—very feminine, but, I thought, she's not delicate. Black sweater and jeans, boots. A gold wedding ring on the wrong hand, a turquoise watch band, the kind you get in Arizona. I had no idea what I wanted to say to her, but it seemed important to make contact—right at that moment I wanted to talk to someone. That's all I can say about my motives, but as I write this, I'm not sure if this is the truth. There was no attraction, not on either side. As I said, she was pretty, but she looked at me as if I were a freak, at least that was how it felt to me, and her manner limited anything I might have felt about her. We can be attracted to people without the attraction carrying a hint of the physical. When she started to talk about Cambodia my soul shifted inside me—and then I was attracted, not as a man is attracted to a woman, but as one person is drawn to another.

When we were in the stairwell and I was seated, Alice let loose with a barrage of Khmer, of which I understood only the words conveying the view that I should mind my own business, leave her alone, and get a life. My command of Khmer was like my command of French—I could pick up a phrase here and there, nothing more. When she was done, she said, in English, "Did you get any of that?"

"Just that you don't like me much and that you think I've been snooping."

"Not even close. More interrogative than declarative, as

in, why were you listening to me earlier today? Just give me
an honest answer."

"I gave you an honest answer a moment ago. That you
were speaking a language I hadn't heard for a long time.
Though come to think of it, that's only half true. The guy
whose truck I patronize speaks Khmer."

"What's the rest?" She seemed to relax a little.

"You interest me. Or, I've been interested in you, sort of
watching you for a while, and not in a creepy way. More
like—what's up with her? She doesn't fit in around here."

"I don't like it. I've been doing my damndest to blend in.
I noticed you once or twice, the cane and the presumption
you were a vet—you look like one—but why would you
notice me? I'm just another grad student."

"You're too old for one thing. And you're, I don't know
how to put it, you look like you know some things, like
you've been around"

Alice didn't say anything.

I tried again. "Look, you can talk to me if you want. Or
not. I just wanted to make contact. Probably not a good
idea, and I apologize if I've upset you."

"It's too weird, this conversation. But I admit that
when I got back from Phnom Penh I was shaky for a long
time..I'm still not myself, whatever that means."

"I get it."

"I bet you do. More so than me. I don't want to feel sorry
for myself. But yeah, I was hurting when I got home. I disappeared for a while when I was in Cambodia. I told everyone
I'd been kidnapped, and I had, but it was a partial truth.
That was six years ago, a lifetime, but not long enough."

"You're still hurting. Maybe a little paranoid?"

"No, not paranoid—I hate that word. I'm touchy."

I knew the feeling. Years ago I didn't sleep. The Veterans sent me to a counselor. It didn't help. And here was someone else who needed a cure, or so I supposed.

"Tell me."

I thought she might walk away, but I was quiet and that usually works. Those with something to say want to fill the silence.

So she told me a story about her life. Just one, about her mother. I listened carefully and forgot nothing. And then she told me another.

—⁂—

What would a ghost look like? It you could see it, would it be a ghost? Probably not. Ghosts are "spirits" and our bodily senses are not able to perceive that which is immaterial. The Vietnamese I knew during the war were all Buddhists. They practiced Mahayana, and believed strongly in the presence of bodhisattvas. But "presence" is a word whose meaning shifts from place to place. Unfettered beings are not a presence in the ghostly sense. Alice believed in ghosts—she saw them—but they were the spirits of human beings, Cambodian persons whom she had known when she lived in Phnom Penh.

—⁂—

"They sent me out into the provinces, to gather information. Just me and a driver. I thought about it for a long time afterward—why did they send me, or anyone? The guy who ordered me to go—not that I didn't want to or was afraid, just puzzled by the request—said it was a 'fact

205

finding' mission. I don't have to tell you that no facts needed to be gathered. By then it was clear that the Khmer Rouge would take the capital. That they had won. So what 'facts' was I supposed to be finding? And we knew enough by then to be sure they would kill me and my driver if I came across them, so I had to wonder what the point really was. I figured it out one day when I was back in the States. I was all alone in D.C., working out my final months and getting ready for something new. And it just came to me on a cold morning that I was supposed to be captured, that my being taken was part of a scheme somebody had proposed deep in the heart of Langley."

"Could be, I mean, you would know better than I. But it happens. What were they up to?"

"They told me the truth. It was facts they were after. Nobody really knew what the Communists would do once they were in power. I wasn't anybody important. What if they shot me? That would tell you something wouldn't it? Instead, they took me on a tour, into the jungle, they showed me what Angkor would be when they had won the war and liberated the country."

"And it was hell."

"Hell on earth. Their idea of heaven was a sane person's idea of hell."

"Sanity was in short supply in those days. I knew a guy who shot at everything that moved. Monkeys and birds and water buffalo and civilians. 'Once everything's dead we can all go home' was his reasoning.."

"If everyone is dead the world can be anything you want it to be. Buddhists believe that suffering is the precondition for the ending of suffering. I heard that in Cambodia all the time, the Revolution was Rama and every act of renunciation proves one's devotion to him."

"Tell me what you saw."

Alice nodded. I had thought she would resist telling me, but she was into the story now, she had to tell someone.

"They took me into the forest. Half a dozen men. Boys really. They were grim and dull, empty faces, big guns in their hands, acrid with sweat. I didn't speak of course; I assumed they were going to shoot me—why shouldn't they? Maybe that would give someone a reason to bomb Phnom Penh, or to lay waste to the sanctuaries, or justify aid to…whom? The situation was a mess—Nixon was out, we didn't have an interest any longer except to save face and to do whatever we could to undermine the Vietnamese. So I walked into the forest waiting to be killed. We walked in silence all day. Six or seven hours, without stopping. They gave me a few swallows of water. At dusk we came to a camp—sixty or more armed men and a few women, cooking fires, more weapons— mortars and RPGs and caches of ammunition. It was filthy. That was what struck me—it looked like no other military facility I'd ever seen, it reeked of waste, garbage and open latrines, there were flies everywhere. I gagged on the smell and on my fear. I was alone in this place that was no place and it was grim and hellish, I might even have thought 'this is what hell is like,' but I was wrong because it was months before real hell was created by these same soldiers, hell for their own countrymen, and by that time I was gone."

Alice stopped talking and went out of the stairwell and returned a minute later with a loose-leaf binder.

"Look inside."

Inside the book were plastic sleeves, and in each sleeve was a photograph of men and women posing, expressionless, also pictures of ordinary scenes, of children mostly, but also of whole families.

"What are these?"

"They were given to me when I was in Thailand. Handed to me by refugees, people looking for their husbands or wives or children. Missing people. Now we know they are all dead. I have hundreds of these pictures. I saved them for reasons I don't understand."

"I understand. I collect pictures too. Not of Vietnam, but other places like it. They put me in the frame of mind I need to be in to stay focused on my task."

"And what is that?"

"I suspect the same as you. Not forgetting."

Alice said, "They were shooting people. Just outside the camp there was gunfire. I could hear it the moment we arrived. Steady bursts of automatic weapon fire, rolling through the forest. I knew what it was right away. One of the cadres took my arm and led me through the camp toward a clearing. The trees had been hacked down and pushed outward to create an enormous circle. There were posts from the hacked trees standing like guards around the circle. And there was a pit in the center, a smaller circle, a deep hole, as if a meteor had struck the spot and tidily etched out this circle. Of course I thought they would shoot me. But instead they brought me to the edge of the pit and had me look into it. Lines of peasants, I suppose they were peasants, they were nearly naked so they could have been shopkeepers or teachers, anyway they were being taken to the clearing and shot. Never mind the details. I turned away, but the soldiers made me turn back, they pushed me toward the pit. I asked them why? The boy holding my arm said, '*Youn*,' Vietnamese. But they weren't Vietnamese. They were Cambodians. After a few minutes they took me back through the forest to the camp. When I got there they left me alone. They ignored me. If I wanted food I had to beg for it from the soldiers. They didn't touch me, or speak to me. Then on the last day I was taken into another part of the camp and presented to Ta Mok. It was him. He told me his name. He asked if I had been treated well but didn't wait for my answer. Then he made a speech about the glorious revolution of the Khmer people, about Angkor, the future of socialism, peasant democracy, on and on, just nonsense. It occurred to me for the first time that they weren't going to kill me. I was being given a message to take back to Phnom Penh. I was a witness to history—he said that—he said we are making history here."

"He wasn't lying."

"I suppose. That's what history has come to—power seized at the point of a gun."

"Not quite that. It isn't what history has come to; it's what we've come to. In Vietnam I saw it up close. We'd go out and blow up things, as if the act of destruction alone counted as a moral act. It's what made us exceptional—not that we could destroy other people, but that we were willing to do so."

Alice thought about this for a moment. "Maybe. I don't have any theories about what I saw. The only thing

I care about are the victims. The perpetrators. . . I don't think about them anymore." She opens the binder again and pages through it, not looking at me as she does so. I thought: I'm the opposite. I only want theories; I can't think about the victims.

I said, "I see the faces but I don't, if you know what I mean. You know why?"

"Yes I know."

"Tell me."

"You're hiding, that's obvious. You feel guilty. I know that because I feel guilty too. But I bet your guilt is more focused than mine, tangible."

"That's right. I volunteered, three times. Three years of it, and six months in Cambodia. If I think about it—you see, I say 'it' and that's the best I can do—if I give in to the memories I can't have a life. And so, yes, I hide here day after day spinning out theories of history or something, writing compulsively, hiding myself within walls of ideas."

"It wouldn't be difficult to figure any of that out. Someone with a conscience—what is he supposed to do? Forget it? They debrief you, but they don't erase your memory. I respect you. I'm not as calm as you are, or as sure of myself."

I laughed and lit a cigarette. "Sorry but I need to smoke. And I'm not calm. I'm contained."

"My mother just died. My father is ill. They think he had a heart attack. I have to leave for home soon."

"I'm sorry."

"Let's go outside, okay? I need some air."

"Sure."

I'm looking back on this event, thirty years after the fact. Thirty years have flown past and in those years I have lived several lives—everyone does. You don't notice how time feels while you're inside of it, and you can never manage to focus enough to really commit events of the moment to memory.

"Alice suggested at this point that we go outside for some air. I was grateful to have the extra time to talk to her. We walked for a short while–it was cold and windy–and I asked her to have a cup of tea with me at the Bengal Palace on Walnut. So we went."

I'm lucky to have that note. It's like a photograph of that afternoon. The 'Bengal Palace,' those sounds, evoke the tiny restaurant with its stained wine-colored carpet, heavy drapes that kept out the sunlight year round; small tables with white tablecloths and clean glasses—good food, cheap and plentiful.

The cold and the wind and the slate grayness of the sky drove us inside. The restaurant was empty, probably because it was the middle of the afternoon, or perhaps because the Inauguration lent an aura of holiday to an undistinguished Monday.

"The *chai* is excellent, and the curries, if you feel like eating."

Alice nodded as if to say, whatever you want, so I ordered plates of food and a pot of tea.

We sat in silence for a while. One of the waiters was watching a Bollywood film on a small black and white television in the back of the restaurant, and I could hear the lilting roll of Bengali from the open door of the

kitchen. Lines of men in women in bright costumes—
orange spangles and flared blue pants—dancing to sitar
and tabla. Their teeth were unnaturally white. I couldn't
stop looking at their teeth. Alice was quiet then, thinking
about leaving.

"You ever read Walter Benjamin?" I wanted to talk, to
keep her with me a little longer.

"Just the essay on art."

"That's a good one. He also wrote a lot about Baudelaire.
He was obsessed with Baudelaire. He wrote about Paris. I've
been reading a book of his called *The Arcades Project*, about
the construction of modernism in Paris at the turn of the
century—art, architecture, poetry, but also consumer culture."

"Why?"

"Why am I reading it?"

"Yes. Why do you do that? Read random books? Most
people around here are working on degrees or writing
books or teaching—I mean at Penn. What are you doing
exactly?"

"What should I be doing?" I didn't appreciate this kind
of question. I never asked anyone why they did what they
did. Looking back on it now I feel like a hypocrite. I wanted
Alice to tell me her life story but was upset when she asked
me about mine.

"I don't know. Working? You could be a teacher maybe
or work for the veterans. Something."

"I am working. Don't assume that unpaid labor isn't
labor. I don't need money—I earned my keep in the
war—I'm owed. And I can't teach—I never finished
college. And I don't do well around people."

"So you're going to spend your life reading Walter Benjamin?"

"Why not? People do. Professors. And why do you care? Look, Alice, I'm staying alive. That's what I'm doing. And I might do something else someday, but for now this is what I need to do—I need to keep busy."

"Okay. I was wondering is all. You don't meet too many people like you."

"Or like you. What are *you* doing? You're just like me. When a person wants to hide out from things he can't do better than a college—they leave you alone. I was in jail for a while, but I like this better, the library, just writing and thinking."

"You were in jail? Drugs?"

"Why do people assume guys like me use drugs? I hate drugs. No, I beat up my brother-in-law. He had it coming."

"Christ."

"Don't worry, I'm not dangerous or unhinged. I have a bad temper. He was cheating on my little sister. My lawyer argued that I was a decorated war hero and I'd had a flash-back, which wasn't true, but I got off easy. I'm really sorry to be telling you this. I was hoping you might trust me."

"I don't trust you. Why should I? I don't know you."

"Eat some *jhol*. It'll cheer you up."

"It's not bad."

"Do you cook?"

"Of course I cook."

"No, I mean, do you *cook*?"

"In that case, not really. I did some, when I was married. But that's a long time ago."

"Your husband was, what, a government guy?"

"A professor. At Georgetown. A philosopher. He still is, though not at Georgetown."

"And?"

"And nothing. I was his student. We married. I got into some things he didn't agree with. Or, I became impossible. Or he did. Who knows? You married?"

"Who would marry me? No Alice, I haven't had a date since high school."

"You must be lonely."

"Must I be? I suppose I am, though, to be honest, I never feel that way."

"I used to be lonely. For years I felt miserably alone. No more though. I miss my mother. And my father—I don't know, when he's gone I think I'll fall apart. I might already have fallen apart."

"Don't. Why not be my friend? I mean, trust me. I'm not asking anything from you."

"They're kicking me out of school."

"They?"

"The head of the philosophy department. The provost, the President. Hell, I don't know who, but I have to leave. In fact, I'm leaving today. I was just in VP for a peaceful few hours before I drive home."

"Why are they doing that?"

"I wasn't being honest with them. I was supposed to write a dissertation in political philosophy, on Hobbes, connect it to Cambodia, which wouldn't have been hard to do, but then I got involved with the refugees. I've been translating testimonies of survivors of the Khmer Rouge, of the prisons and torture centers. There will be a reckoning someday and the record has to be cleared up. People forget, they lose interest, they die. Justice might come in twenty years, maybe never, but somebody has to preserve the memory of what happened. I've been using this place, the stipend they pay me. They're right to cut me off, but it's inconvenient."

"Justice? You believe in justice?"

"Revenge then. They killed two million people. They came down from the north, peasant boys and girls, like the Red Guards, robots, they starting bombing Phnom Phen. I was in the Embassy. The house of cards collapsed overnight. We were extracted. That's how they put it. Americans in the midst of an enormous infection. Except we were the cause of the thing. They left our Khmer colleagues there to be killed and nobody cared."

"They don't. That's the way it is. They lose interest. They have big plans; they have money and position papers and shitloads of ideology. They have policies and alliances. They lecture one another on democracy and power. They write books that nobody buys—they're pulped and the pulp gets used to write the next set of books on the next crisis. They get distracted by other things. They go to Aspen on ski trips or deep sea fishing. Maybe there's someplace more interesting or a better job. They're empty inside. They get bored."

"That's so glib. '*They're empty inside.*' What does that mean? And who are 'they'"?

"You know who they are. You worked for them. And no, they're not empty. That's shorthand. What I mean is the people who make the policies don't care enough to think about what they're doing. You have to have real commitment to do good. Everything is against it. And if you don't like what I think, don't listen to me. Anyway, I'm a dead man."

"Don't say that. You can't think that. I can't think like that. My husband taught me not to give in to despair. I won't."

"Then don't. I have. That's why I hide in the library. That's why I talk to myself."

"What *are* you doing here? I don't get it."

"Keeping a record. Finding some way to connect the past to the present. Honestly, I don't know. I get up and take the trolley to the library and wander around in the books. I take one down and read it. See where it goes. Then at night I go home. It doesn't sound like much, but I don't hurt anybody, or myself. I don't go to bars or use drugs or waste anyone's time. I'm harmless, invisible. The debris of history."

"That's sad. Why don't you publish something? Write a book."

"Does it seem to you that the world needs more books?"

"I'm going to publish a book. About the atrocities. I knew these CIA guys in Cambodia who trained people how to extract information from suspects. You know what happened—they ended up torturing their own people. That's the sort of thing we did. It gnaws at me—I see their faces, grainy black and white photos of girls and boys waiting to die. Some of them are smiling. And we did it. I am going to remember the truth."

"I hate that. *The truth*. You know the truth?"

"There is a way things are and it matters. It matters more than anything."

"Maybe. I've lost touch with it. That's what I'm doing here."

"So, what about Benjamin?"

"What?"

"You asked me about Benjamin before."

"Oh yeah. I started to say that he paid attention to everything, noticed every detail. And at first I didn't understand that, why he would scrutinize everything so minutely, to the point of obsession. I believed when I started my work here—my own Arcades project—I believed that I had to do the opposite, that the way to make sense of the arcade was to ignore the details, the particulars, and collect generalities. So I started writing out theories. I didn't have enough background to figure out where to start or what method to employ—I had no preconceptions or training—so I decided on randomness. I had a notebook and a pen and a couple of million books at my disposal. So I just picked one off the shelf and read it—not even from the beginning—I just opened at random and read some pages until I found what was important and then I wrote it down. I have maybe five thousand pages of theories. 'Great Human Theories' would be my title, or, 'How We Lied', something like that. And I kept at that for a few years. Theories. We are God's creatures, or we are self-made, or history contains meaning, or history is bunk, or the self is sublime....on and on. God and man and the world and truth and meaning and mind. The same ideas spun out in slightly different ways, progress in the spinning or no progress depending on how you read the story. The *City of God* was a big one for me. I spent months going through it, practically copying the whole book out, and puzzling over what it meant. I was elated, walking on air. The seriousness of the book, the certainty of the language—I thought I'd found it."

"It?"

"The answer to the question. The one question I had been asking since a week after I arrived in Vietnam back in '68. The question I thought about every day, on patrols, in my hidey holes, slogging through the jungle. And then in the hospital and home again. I know it sounds strange to put it this way, but I was a kid really, I didn't know anything, and I wanted to understand why things had turned out the way they had, not for me, this wasn't an autobiographical question, but for us, for human beings. Why this world of all the possible worlds? It sounds stupid when you ask it this way, flat out, but it's a real question. Why was I asked to kill people I didn't know, and why had so many millions of other men like me been asked to do the same thing? Why so many victims, so much suffering? And here I was reading Augustine and thinking—*he knows*—I was sure the great hieroglyphic of the universe was about to be deciphered, this was my Rosetta stone, the key. It was mad, it was something out of the theosophists or kabbalists—the idea that there is a key to unlock the mysteries of the world. And of course there is no such key and there is surely no answer to my question."

"How do you know that?"

"Not because I didn't find it, if that's what you mean.

What came to me was that the systems were all wishful thinking. Not answers but wishes, or prayers. The systems are stories. What's the difference between Plato and Shakespeare? Can you honestly say that one is philosophy and therefore makes truth claims and the other is poetry and doesn't? That's nonsense. They're both poetry, and both true and false. And when I thought about it some more—and this was over the course of two or three years—the whole notion of true and false evaporated. The distinction gets you nowhere; I mean, it gets you nowhere if your question is a significant one. 'Is it raining?' requires an answer that's true or false, but I wasn't asking if it were raining."

"I understand. But there's something false about the question, or about the way you're trying to answer it."

"Tell me."

"What makes you sure there is an answer to your question, or that it's even *a question*?"

"I thought of that, believe me. I thought of it at the outset of my investigation. I thought that being in a war messed me up and made me think about things I wouldn't have thought about if I'd gone to college or had a job or been married with a family. Why not ask instead what to major in or which job to accept or what readings to have at your wedding? There's no end to the legitimate questions. But the point is, I didn't do any of those things. At nineteen somebody put a rifle in my hand and told me to shoot people with it. So it was natural that I not wonder about majoring in finance rather than marketing. You see? And as to its being a question, well, it was. If I thought 'why am

I doing this, why is this activity legitimate?' then it *was* a question, and one worthy of answer. The only qualification an inquiry requires is to have been made."

"You sound like Philip, like my late husband. Ex."

"Whatever. I'm bullshitting you anyway. The way I pass my time is my business."

"Don't be angry. I was curious is all."

"I'm not angry. I'm like you, touchy. Earlier today I found myself in this weird loop of memories. I was reading something that reminded me of a trip I took to Japan and that reminded me of a trip to Europe and so forth. Then after about two hours of writing down these memories it occurred to me that maybe I'd never been to Japan or Europe. Maybe I'd made the memories up. I just don't know. But while I was having them they were real and pleasant. So that's the honest answer to your question. I'm not trying to solve any problems; I'm just passing my days in the only way I know how."

"Don't we all do that? We just try to find ways to get by. My project has been pointless but engaging. Writing stories about people I never met and telling myself I'm memorializing them. I've known all along that you can't keep a memory alive—that the only memories are those of the living, and that they're inside of people, not in books, no matter how good the books might be. My mother, for example, is alive in me. I mean, she appears to me and I talk to her just like I talk to you. Right after she died I felt her around me, on my body, in my dreams. I saw her in the house where I grew up, in the woods. I wrote about her, but that was for me."

The waiter came with more tea. He cleared away the dishes. The afternoon was ending indiscernibly—without a sun to set it felt instead like a curtain was being drawn. I picked up the check.

"Alice, listen to me. We're the same person. Have you given any thought to what it means to be 'different' from someone else? I'm putting *different* in quotation marks. If you share one experience with someone you're a stranger. But not this experience. I understand what you went through, and I think you understand me. We need to recognize that we have this terrible thing in common."

"Why? Why is it so important to you?"

"Because pretty soon there'll be a thousand of us left, then five hundred, then fifty. Do you see? Imagine we were on a plane that crashed into the ocean. And there were three hundred people and only twenty survived. You can imagine that. It's the same thing here—we're two of twenty. You couldn't imagine a closer connection if you tried. And that has to mean something because if it doesn't, then what we lived through means nothing. I can't accept that."

"It's better if you don't bullshit me. And by the way, what's your name?"

"Wallace. And I'm not bullshitting you. You think I'm coming on to you? Is that it?"

"Not really. But this *fever* of yours, I don't know, it's frightening me."

"Sorry. I'll stop. You want some dessert? They have lassies here. Mango."

"I wasn't hungry to start with."

"I eat a lot. My mother always said I had a tapeworm."

"Wallace? That's an unusual name."

"I suppose. I'm in a group, guys like me. Not recovered. And what I know is that you might not get better, but you survive."

"And now you're what, a man who talks to himself in the library?"

"That's right."

"We are alike aren't we?"

"I want to forget and you want to remember."

"Maybe."

"I don't want to hurt anyone again."

"I appreciate your concern, I really do. For ten years I've been writing down stories, things people who were there in Cambodia told me. They won't let me go back, I can't get a visa. Ten years, here and in Boston, in Paris where some refugees went, in Thailand, I collect stories."

"Thailand?"

"I couldn't get into Cambodia, or Laos, but Thailand was fine, and lots of Cambodians were there. I was in Aranyaprath, on the border, for a year."

"Are you going back?"

"Maybe. Things are up in the air."

"How will you live?"

"Maybe do some translating."

"But you're going home?"

"Yes, I need to go home."

We got up and left the restaurant. It was dark now, maybe six o'clock. We didn't say anything. We walked and ended up at a three-story house a couple of blocks to the west, on Walnut. We went upstairs, walked up three flights, and into her apartment.

January 21, 1981

It's nearly two a.m. Alice takes a glass of wine into her study. The apartment is dimly lit and she is disinclined to turn on the lights. She sits at her desk. On the wall above her are dozens of black and white photographs—the faces of the men and women murdered at Tuol Sleng. Boys and girls. Their faces only a few of the tens of thousands who were taken to the site of Chao Ponhea Yat High School, once a lovely, white-stuccoed building surrounded by palms and bougainvillea, located in a neighborhood known as the 'the hill of the poisonous trees,' an ordinary place in a pretty city that boasted gracious colonial buildings, lively residential neighborhoods, palaces, and impressive government buildings.

For the past four years, during her time ostensibly spent as a graduate student in philosophy, Alice has made up a biography for each person whose picture she owns. She hasn't many photos from the prison, just a handful of faces out of the seventeen thousand dead—a few hundred pictures released by the new regime in Cambodia, the government of Heng Samrin, installed after the Vietnamese invasion of 1979. She was nearly done with the stories.

Alice knew that it was futile to make up lives for dead people, but it was unbearable for her to think of the false lives that were extorted from the prisoners under torture. Each inmate, upon arrival at Tuol Sleng, was stripped of his or her clothing and possessions, and then, through gruesome physical abuse, stripped of their memories—their identities. Young men were forced to confess that they had worked for the CIA from the time they were children. Khmer communists, subject to special treatment, wrote that they had been on the payroll of the American Embassy, or the French, or that they were secretly agents of Vietnam. Only when there was nothing left of the prisoner was he shot—*"I am not a human being, I am an animal,"* wrote one. Alice's mother had taught her that the most important thing we possess is our memory, the place where we store not only our own identity, but the identities of those from whom we are descended, those who have made us who we are. To willfully forget was to cut one's ties to other people; Alice had tried but failed to understand the pain the people in her collection of austere black and white photos must have felt—she made it her mission to imagine and construct identities for each face, to write an obituary for each person. On her trips to Thailand in the late 1970s she had collected testimonies, eyewitness accounts of the atrocities even then being committed by the Khmer Rouge, fragments of stories which she hoped to assemble into a memorial to the dead, and a body of evidence that might be used to bring justice to the victims—if justice were ever to come.

For each face, a new life, a different life.

Prisoners were photographed upon their arrival in Tuol Sleng. Then they were stripped of all their clothing and put into a cell. They were chained to a metal bar in the cell, chained to other prisoners with whom they were forbidden to speak. If they were given any food, it was a tablespoon of rice gruel–not enough to do more than remind them of their hunger. The interrogations began in the morning at 6:45. The prisoner was beaten until he or she could no longer bear the pain. Of course, the prisoner, who was now only a number and condemned to death in any case, would confess to anything. The confessions were essential as they demonstrated that Cambodia was surrounded by enemies and could only be saved by the Khmer Rouge. The beatings were administered by hand, or with whips. Burning the body was permissible, as was waterboarding. Prisoners were beaten with regularity–three times per day. Duch required that confessions be written out 'on clean paper, in black ink, with good calligraphy.' If a prisoner died under torture, his interrogator would be shot. Of 17,000 individuals incarcerated at the S-21, six survived. Even though there was no hope of surviving, hope was kept alive in the prison by the interrogators—as a means of control perhaps, or as another aspect of the terror that lies at the heart of the Party. To say that the Khmer Rouge was cruel or immoral is meaningless. Theirs was a system of brutality so unattached to political or ideological goals that it made the structure of Auschwitz appear the consequence of a rational mind. Tuol Sleng was the black hole of the Khmer Rouge's self-destruction, and of their willful destruction of Cambodia itself. Pol Pot wrote that his revolution was 'clean and pure,' that it was ordained by God, and that it represented the pinnacle of communism's benefits for humanity. The only product of the revolution was cruelty.

The stories Alice made up were sometimes charming, occasionally profound, and always disturbing. Every story had the same ending. Alice understands that no one will publish what she has written. Her work is illegitimate—it belongs to no genre of storytelling: it is truthful falsehood, fictions made up of facts. She has been found out—she is a fraud, but that does not concern her.

Number six, an old man, was the village barber in the tiny hamlet of Svay Ath. Alice has called him Pan Chothy after one of the gardeners at the Embassy, an old man whose son was killed in the bombardment of the city early in April, 1975. Pan Chothy, was born in 1916. His father died when he was a little boy. His mother raised him in an extended family of aunts and uncles, grandparents and cousins. Pan worked the fields from the time he was a child; he attended school and was skillful at arithmetic but he never learned to read. He left school when he was twelve and continued to work in the rice paddies and vegetable gardens of his village. When he was nineteen, he married a girl from a neighboring hamlet—Alice has named her Mai and imagines that she was very beautiful, petite, modest. Mai and her husband built a small hut on the edge of Highway 5, a narrow dirt road that connects many of the hamlets in Pursat province. Pan Chothy rented a tiny parcel of land for his own use and during the busiest seasons of the year—the times of planting and harvest—worked on the land of a wealthy farmer in the nearby village of Osdao. Pan and Mai had four children, one of whom died soon after birth. The family was Buddhist, and would sometimes bring gifts of food to the monks at the pagoda near Osdao. The monks would offer prayers for their dead child. When he reached the age of forty, Pan purchased a pair of barber scissors and a comb—he began to give haircuts to the villagers who could afford the few riels that he charged. He was skillful at cutting hair, and although he continued to work on his own land, Pan was able to stop hiring himself out to the landlords as a day laborer. His sons—for he and Mai had only sons—went to school, and all three learned how to read. He was taken prisoner by the Khmer Rouge in April 1975 as the cadres moved south and east toward the capital. Under torture, Pan confessed to being a spy for the Vietnamese, or perhaps the Laotians, since the time he had left school. He admitted that he hated communism and yearned more than anything else to become a rich landlord. Pan Chothy was executed—shot in the head—at Tuol Sleng on July 13, 1975.

Alice wrote these stories in longhand on legal paper. Some were less than a page, and some were as long as novellas. The people in them were real, had lived the lives of Cambodian peasants or teachers or doctors or government workers, but their lives were otherwise lost, and what remained were their faces, stark in black and white, days, or minutes, before they were murdered.

We are of this world. We arrive and, after a time, we depart, but this is our sole domain. Alice's favorite book was Freud's *Civilization and Its Discontents*. The *malaise* of culture. She had committed sections of it to memory. She had no patience with ideas that glorified the individual—Nietzsche she despised—the diminution of liberty was the basis of human community, and Alice embraced the idea that self-repression is what makes our collective lives possible. She had seen Hobbes' war of all against all first hand and found nothing in it to admire. If personal freedom was the cost of social order—so be it. This world is our doing. There is no God to blame for Tuol Sleng. Monsters like Duch and Pol Pot and Ieng Sary are nothing special—history is full of such figures—shy bookish men twisted by circumstance into killers, youthful and idealistic students of history, peasants to whom someone had given the books of Georges Sorel or Lenin. Alice loathed romantic idealizations of the Self; she hated Hegel and his Spirit, the procession of nationalists who had fought against the long peace of the 19th century—Herder and Fichte and Mazzini and the insufferable Max Schneckenburger whose doggerel Prussian soldiers sang in 1870:

While flows one drop of German blood,
Or sword remains to guard thy flood,
While rifle rests in patriot hand,
No foe shall tread thy sacred strand!
Chorus: Dear Fatherland, no danger thine;
Firm stand thy sons to watch the Rhine

Alice had this verse taped above her desk, next to the photos from Tuol Sleng—a *memento mori*. Damn the Fatherland, and damn the obscene yearning for a nation of one's own and goddamn the love of spilling blood— did these poets and philosophers have any idea what spilled blood smelled like? Alice had seen dead bodies, the villages destroyed in B-52 raids on the Cambodian border, carcasses—hardly human—ravaged by small arms and blowflies, corpses left to rot along the roads, left as a warning by the Khmer Rouge to those who would betray the Revolution. And damn to hell the Revolution, whatever form it took, a monster feeding on the bodies of those it would free. Alice knew that the idealists were cowards— men and women in love with death, their own and others. "In order to save his nation the hero must be ready even to die that it may live, and that he may live in it the only life for which he has ever wished." The only life he has wished for: his own death, and that of countless others. Kill reason, and monsters are born. Goya's great print hung above Alice's desk as well—a poignant reminder of what she had learned.

He told me that I had sad eyes. What a strange thing to say to someone. But he was gentle. Someone I can't know. One of the ruined ones. Talking aloud in the library, talking to himself as if there were no one else in the world. But he wasn't self-conscious or apologetic. What happens to men and women in war doesn't happen at once, but slowly, like cancer. Philip taught me the fragility of ethics. We are over-whelmed by what we experience. He was gentle and aching with loneliness.

Do I have sad eyes? I suppose I do. Sad eyes look like what? Tired isn't sad and old isn't sad. Lifeless eyes? I think I have lifeless eyes. When I was younger I was radiant, that's what my mother told me, *my shining star* she said. She was always kind to me. Dad took me fishing on Saturday afternoons in the summer; I remember the way the worm felt in my hand as I threaded it onto the hook. I hated doing that. The lake was deep red from the rot of leaves. The water was still and sweet. We caught sunfish and bass. My father taught me how to gut them, filet them, and then lay them in a skillet with bacon fat. They look terrible in the pan, blackened by the grease. But the taste was exquisite. At the end of the day we would hold hands and walk through the woods to our house. Mother would have been baking all day, cleaning and washing clothes. The house would smell like fresh bread and starch. Dad would tell her that I had caught the largest bass. Mom would hug me and she smelled like soap and sweat.

How I loved them.

Number 4 Brother had a mother as well, a father. He went fishing with his father and caught a carp. He gutted it and fried it in oil. He hugged his mother. He wept when he was afraid. He was one of the monsters—Ta Mok. How wonderful to live in the forest and dream of a perfect world. To be a god to one's followers. To kill whomever one wishes. My mother baked bread and roasted chickens that we raised. My father cut firewood and harvested mushrooms and cranberries. We lived in a shack, not unlike a Cambodian house—raised on stilts above the boggy barrens. Golden eagles nested in our front yard. My father harvested a deer each November. He salted the meat. It tasted like blood. Brother Number 3 was a monster. He is hiding today in the northern forests, eating wild game, fishing with a crude line for carp. The sky above him is the same as this one—black and deep as the ocean. Ieng Sary. I saw a photo of him as a young boy. Angelic was what I thought. Soft eyes and long dark hair. A beautiful boy. His mother must have loved him very much. His father was proud that his son could read French. That he could win a scholarship to study in Paris. The colonials were sent to Paris to be trained as the agents of the colonizers. That is the way it is done. Instill gratitude to the oppressor. Instead Ieng read Marx and Lenin and Stalin—especially Stalin. There can be no mercy shown to the weak, the deviant, the unorthodox. Death is the cure for difference.

Thoughts come from nowhere. Alice is free to let to her mind wander. There is no one for her to call or to see. She spent part of the afternoon and most of the night with Wallace—that was enough—she won't see him again. He was gentle, but mad. She told him her life's story. He listened for hours, as if he were memorizing everything. Now she is alone again. The phone will not ring. No one is expecting her. Philip is abroad, teaching in Oxford. He has remarried. He has two young children, sons, and his wife is an Englishwoman. Her name is Jane. Alice can hardly believe that her husband is with Jane right now, or perhaps he is teaching, or alone and writing a book about something inexplicable. Philip wrote to her and told her that he was seeking a divorce—would she agree? Of course. If that was what he wanted. The letters took forever to move across the world. The postal service in Cambodia had ceased, but CIA agents came and went bearing bottles of Scotch and correspondence from the World. She signed papers and sent them back to Washington. Philip didn't write to her again. Philip didn't speak to her again, even after her return, even during her convalescence—her 'time in the wilderness'. Jane wrote to her, late in 1976. She wrote and sent a picture of her baby—of Philip's baby. It wasn't a personal note, just a card, the kind of notice you send to distant cousins. We have had a baby boy. His name is Gabriel. He weights seven pounds, is healthy, and so on. A picture. Alice was knocked flat. Nothing for three years and then this—a child with a head full of black hair. That should be my child was what Alice thought, for about a second, and then, how happy I am that that is not my child. Philip was now beyond reach, and Alice felt nothing but relief. A couple of years had passed, years that Alice couldn't reconstruct, years when she was still on the payroll of the State Department, lived in Washington— in a studio apartment on R Street—commuted to Foggy Bottom and was debriefed on the subject of Cambodia. She was treated respectfully by her colleagues, none of whom had been in the country during the final few years, none of whom had witnessed first-hand the Khmer Rouge victory. It was clear that something terrible had happened in those years, genocide, or perhaps more properly, suicide, as the leaders of Angkor, the absolute rulers of the work- ers' paradise, committed atrocities such as had not been seen for thirty years. Against their own people. This was the mystery that Alice wasn't able to fathom. She could grasp evil—Armenia and Nanking and Auschwitz— but that the Khmer Rouge had turned their murderous ideas against their countryman, killing anyone who wore glasses or who could read or who had a profession—this was an impossible idea, especially because she knew the country, or thought she did, and saw its Buddhist heart, or thought she did—she had been wrong about so much, why not have been wrong about Cambodia as well? She had made mistake after mistake. With Philip, with her political ideas—steeped, she now understood, in self-regard—with her sordid friendships, the waste of her intellect, maybe not that, perhaps there hadn't been so much intelligence after all, perhaps she'd been flattered by the attentions of a bright man and mistaken his admiration for qualities she lacked. What was she after all, now especially? A former low-level State Department operative, now unemployed, an ex-grad student without a degree, an amateur instructor with no interest in teaching, a divorcee with an emptiness in her heart, a daughter without a mother and, she supposed, a father. It was as the Buddhists taught—all is emptiness and illusion.

After her return to the United States a year passed without her being aware of its having done so. Time has meaning when it is filled by something; empty time leaves no clear impression of its passing. Alice was numbed by Washington, by the normality of the streets and the predictability of her life. Philip was gone of course, out of touch. She called his department chairman at Georgetown and all she would tell Alice was that Philip had resigned a year before and taken some time off. He might have gone to England. Or to Paris. Alice realized that the woman had instructions not to tell her anything more precise than this—that much seemed clear from the evasive responses she was given. Then again, she may have misread the situation. Trauma does that to one. She kept seeing the bodies. There were often nights she awoke soaked and reeking of fear, calling out—something. She went home for a week, but left feeling out of place. Her parents had been solicitous and refrained from asking their daughter questions about Cambodia—they only wondered if she were all right, if she would perhaps remain with them. Alice found herself 'at a loss,' meaning that she couldn't conceptualize a normal existence—every daily activity seemed to her a tedious chore, she became 'flat'—these were her ways of describing to herself how she felt. After a few days she knew it was no good. She was depressed—that was a given—but most of all she wanted to be by herself. She said goodbye to her parents and said she would be back soon. They were, she saw, heartbroken, but so was she, and she could do nothing for them.

Back in her Washington apartment, Alice kept away from people. Small talk was out of the question. She tried to read but couldn't focus. She went to the National Gallery, a place she had always loved, and found herself staring at the same fifteenth-century altarpiece for hours at a time; she could look at nothing else but the cracked surface of the depiction of the sheep and the goats—the saved and the damned—the Madonna and Child, the Crucified and broken Christ hung between thieves. Mostly she sat in her apartment and stared at the walls. She corresponded with Khmer-scholars in America and did her best to understand what was going on in the country now that Pol Pot was in power. She got permission to travel to Thailand and interview refugees. As the evidence accumulated, her credulity gave way to conviction. The rulers of Democratic Kampuchea were killing their people.

She went to back to Thailand on her own, without permission. Ragged, half-starved people, many women with children, who had wandered through the countryside for weeks, told stories of whole populations on the move—from the towns into the countryside, from one region to another—and of executions, torture and mass graves. The repetition of testimony soon persuaded even those inclined to view the Khmer Rouge as 'liberators.' No one could stop the genocide.

Now, on her last night Philadelphia, Alice found the meaning of the Buddha's great 'no'. While the wheel of cosmic life continues to turn, the tiny wheel of her corporeal existence had ceased turning, or it had turned full circle. 'Energies take another form.' In the small pool of light cast by her desk lamp, surrounded by the artifacts of her project, remembering the hands of a man on her body—the first time she had been touched in years—remembering relief she felt for those few minutes—just at this moment she reached *nirodha*, the end of her thirst.

Her sabbatical was over. It was time to go home. Alice finished her wine and thought about getting another glass, but didn't move. She thought that she might cry and tried to do so, but after a moment gave up the effort. It is unseemly to weep for oneself and pointless to weep for the dead.

VI.

Albuquerque
February 10, 2012

This is the best I can do. My notes are full of holes, my memory imperfect. One can only make up so much of a story before it becomes fiction and therefore of no value. Though I once had my doubts, I now see that nothing in this world matters so much as the truth—of that I am certain. The liars and dreamers have usurped memory, destroyed the past and turned the present to myth. I don't want to pretend that I know what Alice said or did on that last night she spent in Philadelphia. As I said, she wrote to me, told me a great deal about her life, shared some of her writing—her biographies, including the one quoted here—but I've already made up too much and there is a danger that I'll turn that single day into yet another lie.

We all know what happened in the wider world. The truths of history are available to us now in many forms, though we have the option of ignoring them.

After the day I spent with Alice I took some time off from the library to think about what I might do next. Being with her those few hours destroyed my equanimity, my contentment. I felt lonely for the first time in years. I think I went back to my mother's house, but that was no good either—you can't impose on people, even those who care most for you; you have to make your own way. I know that eventually I returned to my apartment and to the life I had been living, trying to forget Alice—which I did, and surprisingly quickly—and the New Order in Washington. I didn't read the paper or listen to the radio—I read my books and filled more notebooks with what I was thinking about, what haunted me. Those notebooks, now here on my table, are sometimes inscrutable. The worse things got outside of the Van Pelt the more completely I would submerge myself in its books.

Then, in 1984, I took a plane from Philadelphia to Miami, from Miami to Tegucigalpa, and from Tegucigalpa to Managua. This period of my life is crystal clear—I did no reading at all during the six years I lived in Managua, though I did write hundreds of pages of notes on what I witnessed and what I did. But these events, however portentous for me and for the country I came to love, are not relevant here. I think it was in Nicaragua, on a day when I saw a school bus blown up by a landmine manufactured in Pennsylvania, assembled by Americans in a small town not far from where my mother once lived, that I decided to return home and to draw over my life a blanket of forgetfulness, to quit the world once and for all.

In the end, the answer to every riddle is the same—there is no answer. The world never tires of setting problems for us, presenting situations that we must try to understand, but as Alice told me thirty years ago, it is foolish to think we have any control over events, or that understanding has any value. "That's an outdated idea," she told me, "that knowing the answer to some question gives us control over anything. Understanding is the same thing as looking out a window on a winter morning. You see the trees and the sky, but they have nothing to do with you. Nor you with them. The world carries on without us, and the sooner we understand our inability to change anything the better off we are." I had complained that this quietism was just what the liars wanted—they wanted passivity and disengagement. I don't remember what else was said on this subject, but I do know that I continued to believe that at some point in my life things would change, or that I would. I never did, and the riddle remains unsolved.

Acknowledgments

I want to make it clear that this book is fiction. I trust that all readers expert in the history of Cambodia and of the Cambodian genocide will forgive any errors of fact and judgment.

For information on Pol Pot and the Khmer Rouge I consulted many books; these volumes proved most useful: David Chandler, *Voices from S-21: Terror and History in Pol Pot's Secret Prison*; Philip Short, *Pol Pot: Anatomy of a Nightmare*; Ben Kiernan, *How Pol Pot Came to Power* and *The Pol Pot Regime: Race, Power, and Genocide in Cambodia Under the Khmer Rouge 1975-1979*; Elizabeth Becker, *When the War Was Over: Cambodia and the Khmer Revolution;* Vann Nath, *A Cambodian Prison Portrait*; Nic Dunlop, *The Lost Executioner.*

David F. Noble taught me how to think about the ways in which politics shape our lives. His intellectual rigor, deeply skeptical view of power in any form, and his compassion for history's victims continue to inspire me.

My thanks to Marc Estrin and Donna Bister for their support, professionalism, and commitment to publishing writers who might not otherwise have an opportunity to find readers.

Mike Keith, Peter Nash, David Gutierrez, Annika Levy, Hugh Himwich, Cynde Moore, and Florence Goulesque: thank you for your friendship and support.

Brigid read this book before anyone and takes care of everything that is important in our lives. Without her there would be no books.

I hope that my daughters will read and enjoy this rather sad story, that they will read lots of other (and better) books, and that, someday, they will write their own.

Image Credits

Page 1: By Source (WP:NFCC#4), Fair use, https://en.wikipedia.org/
w/index.php?curid=56848099<By%20Source%20
(WP:NFCC#4),%20Fair%20use,%20https://
en.wikipedia.org/w/index.php?curid=56848099>

Page 4: https://en.wikipedia.org/wiki/Kang_Kek_Iew#/media/
File:Kang_Kek_Ieu.jpg, Made available under a Creative Commons
Attribution-Share Alike 4.0 International license
(https://creativecommons.org/licenses/by-sa/4.0/deed.en)

Page 46: WWII: HAMBURG, 1943. People walking along the Grosse
Bergstrasse in Altona, Hamburg, Germany, following the Allied
bombing of the city on 25 July 1943. Photograph. Full credit: Erich
Andres - ullstein bild/Granger, NYC — All rights reserved, used by
permission from Granger Historical Picture Archive, Brooklyn, NY.

Page 55: "Auschwitz Death Camp" axelle b. Made available under a
Creative Commons Universal 1.0 license https://creativecommons.
org/publicdomain/zero/1.0/
https://www.publicdomainpictures.net/en/view-image.
php?image=150632&picture=auschwitz-death-camp

Page 233: "Tuol Sleng Genocide Museum" Copyright © Clay
Gilliland 2013. Made available under a Creative Commons
Attribution 2.0 license
(https://creativecommons.org/licenses/by/2.0/)

Page 238: "The sleep of reason" By Francisco Goya, Public Domain,
(1799) image #43, "El sueño de la razón produce monstruos.
https://commons.wikimedia.org/w/index.php?curid=1783356

About the Author

George Ovitt lives in New Mexico.

Fomite

About Fomite

A fomite is a medium capable of transmitting infectious organisms from one individual to another.

"The activity of art is based on the capacity of people to be infected by the feelings of others." Tolstoy, *What Is Art?*

Writing a review on Amazon, Good Reads, Shelfari, Library Thing or other social media sites for readers will help the progress of independent publishing. To submit a review, go to the book page on any of the sites and follow the links for reviews. Books from independent presses rely on reader-to-reader communications.

For more information or to order any of our books, visit:
http://www.fomitepress.com/our-books.html

More Titles from Fomite...

Novels
Joshua Amses — During This, Our Nadir
Joshua Amses — Ghatsr
Joshua Amses — Raven or Crow
Joshua Amses — The Moment Before an Injury
Jaysinh Birjepatel — Nothing Beside Remains
Jaysinh Birjepatel — The Good Muslim of Jackson Heights
David Brizer — Victor Rand
Paula Closson Buck — Summer on the Cold War Planet
Dan Chodorkoff — Loisaida
David Adams Cleveland — Time's Betrayal
Jaimee Wriston Colbert — Vanishing Acts
Roger Coleman — Skywreck Afternoons
Marc Estrin — Hyde
Marc Estrin — Kafka's Roach
Marc Estrin — Speckled Vanities
Zdravka Evtimova — In the Town of Joy and Peace
Zdravka Evtimova — Sinfonia Bulgarica
Daniel Forbes — Derail This Train Wreck
Greg Guma — Dons of Time
Richard Hawley — The Three Lives of Jonathan Force
Lamar Herrin — Father Figure
Michael Horner — Damage Control
Ron Jacobs — All the Sinners Saints
Ron Jacobs — Short Order Frame Up
Ron Jacobs — The Co-conspirator's Tale
Scott Archer Jones — And Throw Away the Skins
Scott Archer Jones — A Rising Tide of People Swept Away
Julie Justicz — Degrees of Difficulty
Maggie Kast — A Free Unsullied Land

Fomite

Darrell Kastin — Shadowboxing with Bukowski
Coleen Kearon — #triggerwarning
Coleen Kearon — Feminist on Fire
Jan English Leary — Thicker Than Blood
Diane Lefer — Confessions of a Carnivore
Rob Lenihan — Born Speaking Lies
Douglas W. Milliken — Our Shadows' Voice
Colin Mitchell — Roadman
Ilan Mochari — Zinsky the Obscure
Peter Nash — Parsimony
Peter Nash — The Perfection of Things
George Ovitt — Stillpoint
George Ovitt — Tribunal
Gregory Papadoyiannis — The Baby Jazz
Pelham — The Walking Poor
Andy Potok — My Father's Keeper
Frederick Ramey — Comes A Time
Joseph Rathgeber — Mixedbloods
Kathryn Roberts — Companion Plants
Robert Rosenberg — Isles of the Blind
Fred Russell — Rafi's World
Ron Savage — Voyeur in Tangier
David Schein — The Adoption
Vince Sgambati — Undertow of Memory
Lynn Sloan — Principles of Navigation
L.E. Smith — The Consequence of Gesture
L.E. Smith — Travers' Inferno
L.E. Smith — Untimely RIPped
Bob Sommer — A Great Fullness
Tom Walker — A Day in the Life
Susan V. Weiss —My God, What Have We Done?
Peter M. Wheelwright — As It Is On Earth
Suzie Wizowaty — The Return of Jason Green

Poetry
Anna Blackmer — Hexagrams
Antonello Borra — Alfabestiario
Antonello Borra — AlphaBetaBestiaro
Antonello Borra — The Factory of Ideas
L. Brown — Loopholes
Sue D. Burton — Little Steel
David Cavanagh— Cycling in Plato's Cave
James Connolly — Picking Up the Bodies
Greg Delanty — Loosestrife
Mason Drukman — Drawing on Life
J. C. Ellefson — Foreign Tales of Exemplum and Woe
Tina Escaja/Mark Eisner — Caida Libre/Free Fall
Anna Faktorovich — Improvisational Arguments
Barry Goldensohn — Snake in the Spine, Wolf in the Heart
Barry Goldensohn — The Hundred Yard Dash Man

Fomite

Barry Goldensohn — The Listener Aspires to the Condition of Music
R. L. Green — When You Remember Deir Yassin
Gail Holst-Warhaft — Lucky Country
Raymond Luczak — A Babble of Objects
Kate Magill — Roadworthy Creature, Roadworthy Craft
Tony Magistrale — Entanglements
Gary Mesick — General Discharge
Andreas Nolte — Mascha: The Poems of Mascha Kaléko
Sherry Olson — Four-Way Stop
Brett Ortler — Lessons of the Dead
Aristea Papalexandrou/Philip Ramp — Μας προσπερνά/It's Overtaking Us
Janice Miller Potter — Meanwell
Janice Miller Potter — Thoreau's Umbrella
Philip Ramp — The Melancholy of a Life as the Joy of Living It Slowly Chills
Joseph D. Reich — A Case Study of Werewolves
Joseph D. Reich — Connecting the Dots to Shangrila
Joseph D. Reich — The Derivation of Cowboys and Indians
Joseph D. Reich — The Hole That Runs Through Utopia
Joseph D. Reich — The Housing Market
Kenneth Rosen and Richard Wilson — Gomorrah
Fred Rosenblum — Vietnumb
David Schein — My Murder and Other Local News
Harold Schweizer — Miriam's Book
Scott T. Starbuck — Carbonfish Blues
Scott T. Starbuck — Hawk on Wire
Scott T. Starbuck — Industrial Oz
Seth Steinzor — Among the Lost
Seth Steinzor — To Join the Lost
Susan Thomas — In the Sadness Museum
Susan Thomas — The Empty Notebook Interrogates Itself
Paolo Valesio/Todd Portnowitz — La Mezzanotte di Spoleto/Midnight
in Spoleto
Sharon Webster — Everyone Lives Here
Tony Whedon — The Tres Riches Heures
Tony Whedon — The Falkland Quartet
Claire Zoghb — Dispatches from Everest

Stories
Jay Boyer — Flight
L. M Brown — Treading the Uneven Road
Michael Cocchiarale — Here Is Ware
Michael Cocchiarale — Still Time
Neil Connelly — In the Wake of Our Vows
Catherine Zobal Dent — Unfinished Stories of Girls
Zdravka Evtimova —Carts and Other Stories
John Michael Flynn — Off to the Next Wherever
Derek Furr — Semitones
Derek Furr — Suite for Three Voices
Elizabeth Genovise — Where There Are Two or More
Andrei Guriuanu — Body of Work

Fomite

Zeke Jarvis — In A Family Way
Arya Jenkins — Blue Songs in an Open Key
Jan English Leary — Skating on the Vertical
Marjorie Maddox — What She Was Saying
William Marquess — Boom-shacka-lacka
Gary Miller — Museum of the Americas
Jennifer Anne Moses — Visiting Hours
Martin Ott — Interrogations
Christopher Peterson — Amoebic Simulacra
Jack Pulaski — Love's Labours
Charles Rafferty — Saturday Night at Magellan's
Ron Savage — What We Do For Love
Fred Skolnik— Americans and Other Stories
Lynn Sloan — This Far Is Not Far Enough
L.E. Smith — Views Cost Extra
Caitlin Hamilton Summie — To Lay To Rest Our Ghosts
Susan Thomas — Among Angelic Orders
Tom Walker — Signed Confessions
Silas Dent Zobal — The Inconvenience of the Wings

Odd Birds
William Benton — Eye Contact: Writing on Art
Micheal Breiner — the way none of this happened
J. C. Ellefson — Under the Influence: Shouting Out to Walt
David Ross Gunn — Cautionary Chronicles
Andrei Guriuanu and Teknari — The Darkest City
Gail Holst-Warhaft — The Fall of Athens
Roger Lebovitz — A Guide to the Western Slopes and the Outlying
                 Area
Roger Lebovitz — Twenty-two Instructions for Near Survival
dug Nap— Artsy Fartsy
Delia Bell Robinson — A Shirtwaist Story
Peter Schumann — A Child's Deprimer
Peter Schumann — Belligerent & Not So Belligerent Slogans from
                 the Possibilitarian Arsenal
Peter Schumann — Bread & Sentences
Peter Schumann — Charlotte Salomon
Peter Schumann — Diagonal Man, Volumes One and Two
Peter Schumann — Faust 3
Peter Schumann — Planet Kasper, Volumes One and Two
Peter Schumann — We

Plays
Stephen Goldberg — Screwed and Other Plays
Michele Markarian — Unborn Children of America

Essays
Robert Sommer — Losing Francis: Essays on the Wars at Home

www.ingramcontent.com/pod-product-compliance
Lightning Source LLC
Chambersburg PA
CBHW060922190726
48286CB00002B/607